To Angel

Love [signature]

Moon Girl

Moon Girl © Copyright 2004 by Jimper Sutton

All rights reserved. No part of this work may be reproduced or stored in an information retrieval system (other than for purposes of review) without prior written permission by the copyright holder.

A catalogue record of this book is available from the British Library

First Edition: November 2004

ISBN: 1-84375-112-7

This is a work of fiction. Names, characters, places and incidents are the product of the author's imagination or are used fictitiously, and any resemblance to any actual persons, living or dead, events, or locales is entirely coincidental.

To order additional copies of this book please visit:
http://www.upso.co.uk/jimper

Published by: UPSO Ltd
5 Stirling Road, Castleham Business Park,
St Leonards-on-Sea, East Sussex TN38 9NW United Kingdom
Tel: 01424 853349 Fax: 0870 191 3991
Email: info@upso.co.uk Web: http://www.upso.co.uk

Moon Girl

by

Jimper Sutton

UPSO

For my Wife
Pen and Maz

Chapter One

The warm early May sun glinted off the back of my spade as I cleaned my boots of the clay clinging to them, I watched the girl cantering up along the fence that separated our farm from her father's land, a girl of the early sixties, five feet nine inches tall with jet black hair that hung forty-four inches lower than her sun-tanned shoulders, her small dark eyes missing nothing. Riding bareback in a short blue skirt that was torn and tatty and showed a lot of her perfect leg, her upper body clad only in a red silk neck halter that somehow managed to keep her well shaped womanhood in place. She reined up on the opposite side of our boundary fence and looked at me and smiled.

"Buried a dead sheep or your mother?" as if trying to be funny and make conversation to someone she had never spoken to before; although we had seen each other many times over the last twelve months, neither had spoken to one another. Throwing her arm into the air and a wave from me had been the only recognition that we had seen each other. Now here before me, lying over the neck of a superbly fit animal, was this Kentish girl trying to engage me in conversation. She knew a lot about me and that's more than I could say for her. I knew of her, as her father owned and farmed the land alongside us. Her name was a mystery though, but that was soon to be made evident as she swung her leg over the pony's neck and sprang effortlessly to the ground.

"Hi. I'm Mandy, and you must be John."

"Hello. Nice to meet you."

"Oh, you had to meet me," she responded. "I have to meet

everyone you know. John's such a common name. My little brother is called that. I'm going to call you Ox. You have the look of a hefty sort and I like strong men."

The hair on the back of my neck stood up. She liked her men on the hefty side and I was conscious that my shirt lay over the fence were I had tossed it while digging the hole and she was looking at my naked chest, 'but she is only a girl,' I thought to myself. Little did I know then of this young seventeen year old, but I had the feeling I was soon going to find out.

"You own a lot of land, don't you?" she said, "go all the way down to the bottom lane."

"That's right. We join up with the turkey farm over there, pointing my left hand over the fields east, and go all the way down to the river that way, and to the bottom lane that way, just under six hundred acres."

"I wish my dad owned more land; he only has one hundred and twenty acres and that is in two separate lots, so I can never ride the whole in one go."

"Well," I said, "I cannot see why you can't ride around our ground, so long as you keep to the headlands and behave yourself."

"Can I? Yes please! You will have to show me the boundaries. I don't want to jump a hedge and find out I'm in someone else's field. They hate me, but I suspect you know all about that."

"No, I never even knew your name until you told me."

"You are sweet," she said. Tossing her hair away from her face where the breeze was curling it from her back, and I thought 'sod having hair that long if it bothered me that much'.

"Can you show me around now? I'll come round."

And with that she jumped on to the animal's back and pulled the pony round and galloped away into the field only to turn and come back at me, then ten feet from the fence she lay forward and stabbed her sandal shod feet into the side of her partner and the pair flew over the fence, to land and turn to face me.

"Come on then, show me please; jump up".

She held out a broken nailed dirty little hand for me to clasp. I took it and hauled myself up behind her.

"Hold tight," she said.

And we sauntered off along the fence to the next field and joined the hedge line that all our other land had as boundaries; this being the only wire on the farm, for once it had been part of a much bigger field until father purchased it twenty years previously to the war.

I sat on unfamiliar territory, having never ridden a horse before, but somehow the young girl put me at ease, until we entered the thirty-acre grass field overlooking the valley towards the town of Tenterden.

"Hold me tighter," She sang out as she spurred her mount on into a gallop. I slung my arms around her little firm soft middle, and hung on for dear life, her hair tangling in my face with the draught. I could see nothing, but the feeling was there, as was the wonderful smell of her sweaty female body, a natural smell sweet and musty. Every time I came down I met the animal's backbone coming up,

"Ouch!" Then the sensation on my arms as her perfect firm breasts stroked me as I held her in a vice-like grip. Her and the pony were enjoying every minute of it. I was terrified! Going down the hill was scary to me; having no control, my fingers kept trying to get a better grip and only found silk and soft flesh along with the stiff little nipples. We stopped at the bottom and she turned her head to one side and looked at me. Those lovely dark eyes met mine.

"You enjoyed every second of that, she said in an impish sort of way. Did you like it? I did!"

I blushed and we spent the next half hour strolling along those dark green hedges bordering the little used lane, with my arms around her slender body enjoying every moment, and climbed back up to the top of the farm into the large old cherry orchard, then into the twenty acre wood that had not been cut for many years, some of the old oaks were hundreds of years old, I was amazed at the way the pheasants and other birds took no notice of the three of us, we plodded along slowly enjoying every moment together, her head turned this way and that, all the time taking in all she saw, and then we arrived back at the wire fence.

"That's it," I said, and slid off my precarious perch from behind Mandy.

"It's lovely," she said. "You will have to make me some jumps in the corners so that I can go from one field into the other without having to go to all the gates. Will you please, please?"

So for the next week, I was engaged every spare hour I had cutting the hedges down and driving stakes in, then cutting a rail to place along the top so that Mandy and David, her love, were able to glide over in safety. I never saw the lass in the next three weeks but on my rounds inspecting the crops the signs were there that the pair had been busy, for quite a path was now being worn alongside all the hedges and on the headlands of the corn where the hooves were cutting up the turf. Also at the point of landing, at a couple of the jumps over the hedges, there was becoming a dust bowl as the grass gave up the struggle to compete with all the disturbance and a covey of partridges along with the pheasants took the area up as a dust bath.

There were many game birds on our land, as we had a local shoot that rented the ground and the thought did cross my mind that perhaps they would not be to happy with me for inviting the sister of the biggest known poacher to ride the area. We owned the land and if they did not like it, 'tough'. Then one night on my visits to the local pub, a friend of mind the son of a builder, caught up with me, took me aside and over a pint gave me a warning.

"I see that Mandy has taken to riding around your farm; we were working up that way the other day on a roof and saw her on your land. She said you had given her permission to ride the whole farm. Soon you will have a gypsy camp if you don't watch it. Be careful John. You know what she's like."

I looked puzzled; I had no idea and said,

"No."

"You don't know? Everyone knows her reputation, and her mother, watch out for her my boy. She will murder you!"

"What are you going on about?" I said.

"You don't know our Mandy's reputation?"

"No!"

"Poor sod. Have you never been with her on your own?"

"Only ridden around on the back of her pony once. Never seen her since."

"Bloody hell, you're lucky! If ever they find out. Look out, here comes Jeff!"

And with that he quickly moved away and engaged Jeff in conversation, and by the look of the glances my way, I was the topic of conversation.

I found Eric and played darts thinking no more about the subject until I got home and was in bed; then Alan's words came back to me. Watch out for her mother and beware of Mandy, for she had a reputation. I was intrigued and wondered what he had meant; he had said it more as a warning than just idle talk.

I had seen Mandy's mum many times in the weekly market; a big woman with long black unkempt hair of very fair proportions, always dressed in a thick pullover and long skirt, wearing rather large floppy rubber boots, a typical dairy farmer's wife who could strip the milk from a cow's udders faster than any machine. Seldom with Mandy's dad, whom I knew, as we had often chatted over the hedge, or when he had borrowed a bit of farm machinery to help him make hay, he kept a dairy herd of Friesians and the milk stood outside the gate of the farm in churns every day, up on their old wooden railway sleeper stand awaiting the collection lorry to take it to the dairy.

And of Mandy's reputation 'I must know more,' I thought to myself. What could it mean? I had to find out, but how, for I seldom saw the girl although the well-worn tracks around our farm told their own story. Someone was riding around the land; I must keep my eyes open more. During the next week I asked all my mates if they knew anything of the girl and all the information

I got was that she went to school in Ashford or somewhere like that to an all girls school. I had to find Alan, as to my mind he knew more of the girl than he let on, and he had shut up like a trap as soon as Jeff showed his face.

Next day I drove into the yard of the builders' merchants to see if I could locate Mr. Aldridge's son,

"Hello," I said, as the foreman of the yard came out to see whom it was arriving.

"Have you seen Alan, Mr. Aldridge's son?" I enquired.

"Saw him this morning; gone out on a job. Did you want him for something?"

"No, only to ask him a few things."

"Sorry, can't help, but can I give him a message when he comes back?"

"Yes please, ask him to meet Big John in The Bell later can you please, and tell him it's important?"

"Sure will", and he turned and vanished into the office from where he had appeared. I turned the van around and drove home to feed the pigs. At eight pm, I walked into the pub and ordered a drink and as I sat down with some of my mates, Alan came in.

"John, glad to see you. What's the panic? You wanted to see me?"

"Sure do Alan. Let me get that," as he ordered a pint. "Find a seat over there," I said. Pointing to a seat under the window away from the table where our other mates sat. A pint of bitter was placed on the bar and I paid, then walked over to the window and sat beside my mate.

"You remember the other day when you told me to watch out for Mandy, the girl on the pony next to our farm in Kent? What did you mean she had a reputation and watch out for her mother?"

"You mean you really don't know? That girl is big trouble my friend if ever there was, and her mother is a real tartar. I know, my brother was warned off her last year."

"Why? What did he do?"

"That's it, nothing; only sat next to her when they came home on the train every day from school." And he gave a look over his shoulder to make sure no one was listening. "She goes to a posh girl's school; near Ashford, he met her at the station every evening and sat with her, that's all." Alan took a sip of his beer. "Her mother and big brother came to our house and read the riot act. What that woman was going to do to dad and my brother if he kept seeing Mandy is no-one's business." He lay on his arms and put his face in their palms. Mum knows the woman; says she comes from a gypsy family in Essex, took up with her husband when she was only sixteen, and ran away from the family camp to live with Mandy's dad, who was the son of the rich farmer whose farm the family were spud picking on at the time." All the time he was telling me this he was looking around as if to see if any one was listening, he seemed scared just talking of Mandy it did not make sense. "Because of it the dad was cut out of his family's will, and his parents have disowned him, bloody rich they are too. Now Mandy's growing up, they don't want her to go the way her mum did and her big brother is no better. The girls he goes out with! Different one every week, so they say, but poor old Mandy must never look at a boy. I pity the bloke who gets tied up with that lot."

And so the meaning of the warning became clear to me. Mandy was bad news. Their daughter seemed to be out of the market for boy friends. I spent more time after that up our farm away from home every day, finding a reason to go and work in the orchards or do something with the hedges hoping to spot the animal and rider that was leaving the tell tale tracks around our farm. Day after day I spent waiting for any signs of life. It was a mystery. When did Mandy ride around? It got so bad with no sightings, that I placed black cotton thread across one of the gaps in the hedge and next day I looked at two pm after spending the day spraying the apples. The cotton was broken and I never saw a thing so I replaced it with another strand. Again it was snapped when I looked at seven pm the following day. The ghost was somehow moving around with me not seeing it.

The days became weeks and the cherries started to ripen. Someone had to start the bird scaring guns up at first light, and turn them off at dusk, so the local inhabitants could get some peace and quiet; that was the law. We had a man living in the near by village of Stone who started them before the sun got up, and nipped over to stop them as the birds and sun went to sleep.

One day he could not do the evening shift so I elected to do the job, a simple task as one only had to pull the rubber pipe from the gas canisters, to stop the guns from going bang. It was nearly dark as I walked over to the last gun, up under the wood at the far side of the four acres of cherries, when I heard the sound of a horse galloping my way. The evening was hot and sticky, and I had a sloppy short-sleeved black shirt, and a pair of jeans on so was sure she had not seen me in the dusk. I stood back in the hedge, thinking that as I had not seen her, she had obviously not seen me.

Mandy on David came hurtling along the side of the hedge of the orchard. Then her mount saw or sensed me; it shied and the girl fell to the ground. I ran from my hiding place to see if she was hurt. The breath was knocked out of her, but luckily she was OK. Her pony turned and came wandering back to us, and nuzzled its nose into her as if to say sorry. I helped Mandy up and she thanked me.

Then we got chatting, and sat on a large tree stump at the edge of the wood. She asked if I smoked, and showed her pleasure with a kiss on my cheek when I said, "Yes," and handed her a packet of Woodbines. She took a fag and I offered her a light. She took a deep drag, and held the flavour in her lungs, then blew the smoke out over her soft sensuous lips in a long drawn out flow. She was used to tobacco and enjoyed a smoke that was evident by the way she smoked and held the cigarette. The pony browsed on the hazel and hawthorn bushes and Mandy looked into my eyes.

"Thanks for the fag; I have been dying for one all week. Don't let my parents know I smoke please."

"No hope of that," I said, "for I hardly know them."

"Good, keep it that way please, don't let them know I have seen you, as I am not allowed to see men or speak to them, yet I love the company of men, they understand girls like me." 'What did she mean?' I thought to myself, like me? Then Alan's warning came flooding back to me. "BEWARE!"

We sat there on the tree stump and the new moon tried its hardest to cast a glow on earth. Mandy moved closer to me and put an arm around my waist.

"You don't mind do you?" she said, "only I feel chilly not moving around," and we started to talk of horses, which I knew little about.

"You must be clever at something," she said, when I could not name three different types of breed. "I bet you know what an apple is; if I showed you a fruit you could tell me what variety it is."

"Oh yes, easy!"

"See?" she said, "you are clever at some things," and with the same breath asked if I had a girlfriend. The question came at me from out of the blue. We had talked of the latest records out in the hit parade, what crops we grew, how many sheep we owned and all about pigs; then to ask if I had a girlfriend like that surprised me.

"No, not at the moment," I said, and she looked at me and asked if I would like a girlfriend. "Well yes, of course I would," but I seldom had time to go out in the evening. Although I did belong to the Young Farmers' Club, I rarely had a chance to meet girls. Mandy turned to look at me.

"Would I be her boyfriend?" she said, as she fancied me, and had done so since I held her tight on the day I had shown her around the farm a month ago.

And so we lay back on the damp dew sodden grass and started to kiss. She became my girl that night; her warm body with my tee shirt stretched over her to keep both of us warm. Her ample firm breasts warmed the hairy chest of mine. The moon only moved half an inch, across the sky that night before she said she had to go, she had been out for two hours now and her family would start to worry. She said that as she came home from school late every day, the late evenings and moonlit nights were the only time apart from weekends that she could ride, her parents made her do her homework, and all the housework first. So the mystery of why I could not see her riding around the fields was solved; she did it at night when I had gone home.

"I will meet you tomorrow night," she said with a thrill in her voice as she caught her pony up and vaulted across his back.

"See you at nine-thirty then," and kicked the young stallion into gear; then were away into the darkness of the warm, calm evening. 'Boy what a girl! Forty minutes before, I had hidden in the hedge on her approach; now here was I with the mistress of the pony wanting to be my love. Lucky me!

CHAPTER TWO

I was awaiting Mandy long before the sun-set, I had shaved that evening, a rare thing for me to do, and had a good bath; put clean clothes on and given my thick shoes, a good polish. I meant to make an impression on the dark haired girl of David. I wore a new pair of jeans especially for the occasion, along with a green knitted sweater that mum had given me as a Christmas present, a good splash of Old Spice and I was ready.

Now as I sat on the old ash stump awaiting the girl who wore no scent, her body fluids alone made her ooze with appeal to me. Smoking a Woodbine I remembered my hair that I had washed but failed to comb. I pulled my fingers through my tangled locks, hoping to get some kind of neat look to the strands of hair that covered my ears, and thought to myself, that really I should have paid the barber's a visit that day. 'Too late now,' I mused, for surely the pony would show itself soon, and anyway all the barber's shops had closed hours ago.

The startled shriek of a blackbird was the first warning I had that she was nearing me. Then around the end row of cherry trees, this seventeen year old beauty came into view wearing a white blouse, whose buttons only just held it together, her short blue skirt up high on her legs, as she slowly wandered along on her sturdy David. I stood up and she smiled, the biggest evocative smile I had ever seen and stopping, said, "Catch!"

And threw herself from the animal's back for me to stop her fall. My arms caught her and she placed her lips to mine, and we kissed our greeting that evening. She stepped back and tied the reigns to a bough of a tree, then said,

"Do that again," and ran away laughing as she skipped apace from me. I took the hint and chased after her, catching up easily as if she intended me to, and flung my arms around her. Her legs seemed to give way and we both toppled to the ground. She turned to face me.

"I really got it right that first time we met," she said as she stared into my eyes. "You are as strong as an ox. I knew it when I saw you. Please be careful with me; don't mark my body whatever you do. Mum will kill the pair of us."

'There goes her mother again,' I thought. "Why would I mark her? She was not a sheep; surely those we marked not girls. And what was it with her mother? Mandy was frightened something awful of her mother.

"I would never mark you," I said. "Whatever gave you that idea?"

"Nothing really, only I bruise very easily and a friend of mine has love bites all over her neck and she has to wear a roll neck jumper in this weather to hide them from her parents. Please don't do that where it shows; do it there."

And she undid her blouse to reveal a perfect bosom in no need of any garment for support. I lay and studied the form before my eyes. Here she was, a Kentish girl who I hardly knew, baring herself to me as if to invite a kiss. I could not resist or disappoint the girl so gently held her and kissed her, then pulled her blouse together.

"You do fancy me don't you?" she said in amazement.

"Of cours," I said,

"Only you are the first boy to ever cover them up. What's wrong with you? That was lovely what you did."

"Look," I said, "you don't have to throw yourself at me. I do like you as you are."

"But I like it."

"Maybe, but there is a place and time for everything. Look

Mandy, you must not throw yourself at all the boys. Your body is yours. Don't let them play with you as they wish. If they truly like you, they will bide their time and when it's right, then that is OK, but please don't think that if you don't offer yourself to them, they will not like you. I like you, but not for what I can get easily, so button it up, let's be friends, take our time and enjoy each other. Let's cuddle and kiss."

She was staring at me in amazement.

"No boy has ever refused before," she said. "I thought that is all they ever want. Do you mean we will see each other and you don't want me?"

"No not at all, only let's take our time, and then when it is the right time, we can both enjoy it. You don't really like it when a boy uses you then goes away as if you are a rag doll do you?"

"Well it is nice and they do come back to me. If you don't want me, tell me so, don't play with a girl's feelings please because I really do like you Ox."

"You don't get it do you Mandy?"

"Not from you by the sounds of things, no," and I hugged her.

"Come on Mandy; I will show you, and gave her a long passionate kiss and ran my hands up her back, then under the jumper she was wearing and we lay back and the pleasure showed on her face. For over an hour we did no more than lay and cuddled. The pony started to get restless; he tried to reach more palatable fodder along the hedge and tried to pull the reins from the bough. We turned around and parted. Mandy looked at me.

"You Ox are so different from all the other boys; you never tried to get into my knickers but I must go or mum will send a search party out to find me. Please will you see me tomorrow? I've had such a lovely time."

"Of course I will; see you same time here?"

"Yes please, and wait until I tell the girls at school tomorrow, they will be so jealous!" She rose and gathered up the pony, I helped her onto his back and watched as she vanished into the night singing a song aloud to David and any one to hear. Mandy was all right, I thought, willing to go all the way. Steady lad; she was only just seventeen and as she said, had never truly made love to any one, and she insisted in a funny sort of way that I had to believe her'. She was very young but I was nearly nineteen and had to see her more often.

The following night she was late and her attitude was different, more cautious in her manner. She alighted slowly and hesitantly turned to greet me with my new hair cut.

"Ox, what have you done to your hair? It's a lot shorter. I love it," and we embraced and kissed. She seemed more rigid tonight, not so soft as last evening. Then she pushed herself away from me and looked at me.

"What's the matter?" I said.

"Nothing," she said. "I just cannot believe that I have a boyfriend who wants to treat me like you want to," and she burst into tears, real tears, they flowed down her cheeks and she hugged me. "The girls at school said you must be a saint the way you treated me last night and they all want to meet you, only that's impossible."

"Why?" I said, "Can you not let them see me?"

"Mum," she said. "If she knew I saw you, she would kill you. I'm not allowed to see boys because she says they only want one thing, but you don't. All my life she has told me that, then last night I met you and you didn't just want that; you are so odd."

"Oh I do want that Mandy, only at the right time and place. I told you there is more to life than raw sex."

"So you say, but show me; do please, show me."

"Your mother can't be as bad as you say; surely she must let you out sometime."

"No, she will never let me out."

"Why? Does she suspect you of giving yourself away to every boy?"

"Maybe," she said, as she bowed her head in a feign of shame, not realising that all boys do not expect to have it served on a plate the first time they meet her.

"Is there no way we can go out together other than meeting like this?"

"No and if they find out, that's it, so let's make the most of it now."

"Steady on; does your mum always find out?"

"Yes; usually someone phones up or a friend tells my parents, so you see I must make the most of it whenever I can, mum or one of the others are always keeping an eye on me."

"Let's think; is there no way you can go out on your own?"

"No, the only time is when I go to Sally's home for the weekend."

"Sally? Who's she?"

"One of the girls from school; they let me go there but it's out on the marsh, miles from anywhere with nothing to do."

"That's it then; you go to Sally's; I will collect you and we can go to a pub; you look old enough."

"Yes, I love cider," she said, in an eager sort of voice. "Would you buy me a drink, as I am not allowed money?"

"Not allowed? Whatever do you mean by that?"

"I'm not allowed money; mum pays the school fees and she is the only one allowed to handle money in our house. Dad is never allowed to touch it, let alone spend any."

"Why?"

"It's a gypsy thing, don't bother."

"Now Sally; where does she live?"

"Out on the marsh near Hythe. It's over a mile from the road; it's a lovely family. Sally's allowed out if she wants to go; she has a job in the tea rooms at the little railway station at weekends, and always has fags and makeup, but I don't go very often now as Sally's got a boy friend and there is nothing to do, and I love riding. The weekends are the only time I get to do any in the daylight and mum and dad can see me on our farm. The day we met, they had friends of theirs down and had gone out."

"Mandy; see if you can go this weekend and I will see you and we will go out."

"It's no good," she replied, "how can I go out in the clothes I have got?"

"Surely you have something?"

"No, not really; my school uniform, but they will not allow me in a pub in that and if I tried to take clothes from home, mum would want to know why I wanted them."

"Can't you get a skirt or anything out?"

"No, not past mum. You see she is a real gypsy and very suspicious of everything anyone does. Anyway I have exams coming up and must study."

"What are you studying for my love?" I said, and she looked into my eyes and the tears started again.

"Now what?" I said.

"You called me my love," and she hugged me so tight I thought my ribs were going to crack.

"That's the first time anyone has called me my love."

"Now come on Mandy; your mum and dad call you their love sometimes surely?"

"Never, they hate me. Mum hits me and so does dad, and they have never called me 'love'."

"They hit you? Why?"

"I don't know; because I'm a girl and they say girls are no good. I should have been a boy like my brothers."

"That's no reason to hit you there must be more to it than that, no father hits his daughter."

"I'm not his girl really, for after my big brother was born and only one year old mum and dad split up, and mum ran away to find her real family, but dad found her, and brought her back, then I was born and I am not his true blood."

"How many brothers have you got Mandy?"

"Three brothers, and a little sister of six but they are only half sister and brothers."

"A big family then! What are you studying for at school? You see I know nothing of you, not even your surname."

"My name is Mandy Smith; it's my mother's name. Mum would not take dad's name. I'm studying Law."

"My God! You've got a brain then!"

"Of course; did you think I was just a pretty little thing then?"

"No, no, but why Law?"

"I want to give my father what he is owed when I qualify."

"Give what to your dad? How?"

"Look Ox, you don't want to know."

"Yes I do; what is it?"

"No, I'm not saying. One day I will tell you, but not yet."

"Getting back to Sally's; when can you stay there and what about her parents? Won't they tell yours if we go out?"

"Never; they won't even talk to one another now. Sally's mum is nice; she hates my mother and father and never talks to them and as for Sally's dad, he won't even look at my dad, not after what he did."

"Your dad really must have done something; go on tell me."

"No Ox; now cuddle me like last night."

We lay again in our spot under the large old Lime tree, that we together had chosen in the hedge as our love bower. The old tree must have been over three hundred years old and I dreamed of how many courting couples this aged lump of wood must have seen when it was young and the skies above only allowed birds to fly; then man came along with his aeroplane and war. In the last war a doodlebug had chopped off the topmost bough of the giant, to reduce its height and make it spread its arms that we now lay under. The air was cool tonight and we snuggled up close and kissed with the eagerness of youth. We discussed Sally's home and when Mandy could get a night down at Sally's on the marsh. She said she would ask Sally at school tomorrow and let me know. So I had to wait until tomorrow.

I awoke the next morning to a raging gale and thought of the evening to come with the answer from Mandy. Then when the evening came, the rain started to lash down. 'All I need,' I thought. She will not be there tonight on her pony, not in weather like this.

Jimper

I made my way to our farm in Kent and had to park my old car on the road of the yard, the ground was too wet to drive on and we had no tractor up on the farm, I did not fancy getting stuck tonight. I made my way on foot to the old large dripping Lime tree and waited.

The clouds flew across the sky and the rain came in nasty squalls, heavy at times. Then the new moon shone for a second, but Mandy never showed that night, so at eleven I trudged across the orchard and up through the wheat field to the car. The answer about Sally's would have to wait until another night.

The following evening was like summer again and I was sure the girl would come like an angel out of the gloom. At eight thirty I was in place but my heart was left to pound alone. She never came; I began to wonder if her mother had smelled a rat or my Old Spice as I had laid it on rather thickly the other night and it did tend to linger on your clothes, if her mother did not smoke, maybe she had smelt it and Mandy had confessed the cause of having it on her clothes. So I hid up in the branches of the tree in case someone came to find the reason for Mandy's rides at night. I was aware that her mother was a very vindictive woman. The wind shook the leaves in the top of the mighty lime and the drops of sticky nectar found their target on the back of my neck with irritating regularity.

Mandy again failed to show. I walked to the car in the yard, then had the idea that if she did come very late, I would not know, so unlocked the shed and got the faithful cotton reel of black thread. I walked back to the cherry orchard and strung a strand across the hedge and first tree so as to block the whole width. The cotton's tell tale remained intact for three days as I made a frequent visit to check. Then one morning it was gone.

Mandy had been and I had let her down as for the last two nights I had given my night time visits a miss, looking for Alan, to wring more information out of him. But I failed to make contact as he was always out. He had a woman on the go, his mother had told me and only seemed to come in to change his clothes, seldom stopping to eat anything, but she was sure he could not live on love alone.

Later that evening, I went along the headland to wait under our passion tree as we had named it, then as I ducked my head under the outermost canopy of leaves to get under the bough, I caught sight of a bit of paper wedged into the bark it was a note from Mandy that was written in the most beautiful copper plate handwriting.

'Please Ox; come back to me. I am sorry I could not come last night. Your loving Mandy, kiss, kiss.'

The paper was a strip from a spray can that lay on the headland of the wheat field. So Mandy must have ridden around the farm within the last two nights but as the bit of paper was not dated, I was unsure as to how many nights I had missed her. How many times had the lass been disappointed on not seeing me? I felt I had let her down. I sat with my back to the trunk and listened as the starlings went to roost in the birch tops on the other side of the wood.

Then my heart missed a beat. The sound of hooves as the pony came along the side of the orchard. My Mandy in full daylight! The setting sun played a glittering, silent tune, in her flowing, black hair. I crept out from under the canopy of leaves. She saw me and spurred David into a gallop, covering the last eighty yards in record time to pull the mount up in a skidding halt. She flung herself into my arms.

"Darling I missed you; where were you last night?" and kissed me with a tender pair of lips that said more than words could.

"I'm sorry; I waited two nights for you but you never showed, then I gave it a miss for three nights as I was busy."

I lied and felt ashamed that I could not tell her I was trying to find out more of her background. She smiled and gathered the pony's reins up and attached them to an ash pole growing in the hedge twenty yards away. Tonight the sky twinkled with the stars and the old moon had the power to really cast a glow on the leaves and the ripening cherries. Mandy was full of her news. Sally had suggested that next weekend she went from school on Friday and stayed until Monday then went with her to school. Her mother had no objections to her 'going out on the marsh' as she put it, for there she would be safe from any boys. Mandy made me promise that I would take her out to a pub even if she had no proper clothes to wear as Sally was the wrong size for her to borrow anything from. We lay on the ground and I fondled and kissed her. She then started to explore my body with her hands. The sensation was out of this world to me. She seemed so young yet knew what to do.

She said that the couple who lived in the cottage in the bottom lane had told her dad that they had not heard her riding past their home for some time, Mandy was worried her mum would want to know the reason, so she asked if there was any way we could change the course around the farm away from the cottage for she was frightened that her parents would get suspicious if she was gone so long, but failed to cover the distance. I thought for a few minutes but her hand was distracting me as she softly caressed me. "Stop it," I said. "Let me think." The fields along the bottom lane were all down to winter wheat, now knee high, and did not lend themselves to a new ride along the top to join up with the headland of the next field. The only way was to go along the top of the long field, then over the hedge and across the middle of the other one, a distance of ninety yards. I had an idea.

"Mandy, if I drove a tractor from the top across the wheat and made a path, you could miss the cottage by fifty yards and so they would not hear David's hooves." Mandy wriggled with delight she was getting excited at the thought. "But you will have to ride it in the daylight so they see you have a new route. I must do something to the track to make it look as if you had to change. Now why would you have to move your path? I lay on my back lost in thought, "I know; there is an old wire netting fence along that hedge. I will pretend to spray the wheat tomorrow, only I will use clean water and make sure when doing it that the tractor catches the old wire. I could then tow it into the headland, wind it up in the sprayer and then go to the house to ask to borrow a pair of pliers to snip the wire to untangle the sprayer."

"Do you think it will work?"

"Of course. That way they will know why you cannot ride in the dark, for fear of tripping your pony up. I will make the path and a jump for you to carry on with the ride away from their cottage and lane. Leave it to me," and with that we carried on with other things. She was so easy to please and I wondered why other boys did not suggest it without intercourse. It seemed to make her happy to think that at seventeen she was safe with me.

CHAPTER THREE

The subject of the weekend came up again and she really wanted me to go and take her out for the night. She had never been allowed the privilege before and kept on about it. I said I must have Sally's address if I was to find it; the marsh was a big place. She laughed.

"You cannot miss it for it is the only house for miles."

"Yes, but what's her name and address?" She told me Sally's surname and it rang a large bell in my head. "Surely it could not be the same one!" Then she gave me the address. 'Yes, I knew of the place.' I was acquainted with her father; our family had been friends for many years as my father had been a scout leader along with Mr. Wilton, Sally's dad. I could talk to him and maybe he would know the secret of why Mandy was so scared of her mother. But that could wait until tomorrow. Now I had this delicious girl to myself and the moon was high in the sky. A glance at my watch told me that tonight we were going no further. The girl had to get home now and fast! So we untwined ourselves, arranged our clothes and I kissed her good night.

Early next day, at six am, I started the tractor up, hitched the sprayer on and took off to spray thirty acres of two knot winter wheat with water, making sure that I caught the fence, and dragged it into the field, so obstructing the pony's track along the headland and thus making it unfit to ride.

Two hours later Mr. Langridge answered my sharp knock on the cottage door.

"Hello," he said. "What's the reason for this visit so early?"

"I am sorry," I said, "but I have picked up the old wire fence along the hedge; it's tangled around the tractor and sprayer and I have no way of cutting it free. Could you possibly lend me a pair of wire cutters or pliers to free it? It's come away from the hedge for thirty yards and I do not want to pull it any more as it might tangle in the corn. I will have to block the path that the girl uses so she does not ride along there or she could have a nasty accident."

"Ah yes; I have heard her at dusk galloping around on that horse of hers. Nice looking lass, really can ride too. Now, wire cutters, out in the shed!" He walked down the garden path to open the shed door and unhooked a pair of cutters from a nail on the wall. "Hope these will do," he said. "Bring them back when you are ready." I thanked him and vanished. That part of the plan was over; now he would not worry if he did not hear or see the girl riding.

The wire was extracted from the chain and hook that I had used to pull it from the hedge. I roughly cut the wire in half, leaving it strewn across the headland, noting in my head to watch for them when we cut the corn in a couple of months time. Now my hands were put to work making a new jump half way up the field and a path for Mandy to ride. That was the easy bit; three times across the field with the tractor and the wheels ran the green soft corn to the ground, leaving a trail so easy to see. Now with that done it was time to put part two of my plan into action.

I returned the cutters to Mr. Langridge, armed now with an excuse to visit Mandy's house, to warn her parents that the path their girl rode around our farm had been altered for her safety. Never having had cause to go to the house before, my eyes were taking note of everything. The first thing that came to my notice was the untidy state of the whole place. Junk was everywhere, more like a scrap yard than a dairy farm. A couple of horse drawn farm carts stood under an old oak tree, the wheels long rotted away.

Mandy's mother came out of the battered back door as I

approached; it looked as if it had seen better days long ago and I wondered if it was in a fit state to even shut, let alone keep the weather out! The whole place was swarming with rough looking dogs chained to all sorts of anchors, from pegs in the ground to the clothes post and an old plough. Chickens and bantams swarmed everywhere scratching in and around the numerous dung heaps

"What do you want boy? Nothing here for you," said Mandy's mother.

"I'm John from the adjoining farm."

"So what do you want?" She was defiant in her manner and picked up an old broom that stood up against the wall outside the door as if to arm her self with it.

"I came to tell you that the path your girl, I believe that is who she is, rides around on our farm is blocked by some old wire that got tangled in our sprayer and I have moved the course for your child (I thought child sounded better than girl to throw her off the scent) up onto the top headland.

"She's not here; I will tell her. Now go and leave us alone."

I walked back to the tractor and thought, 'What a strange woman.' Alan's warning came back to me. She sure was a witch. A red lamp should be hanging around her neck as a warning to keep away.

Now for part three of my plan. Things were going well so far and I prayed the next part would seal it once and for all. I left the hills and dropped down onto the marsh and home with a clean empty sprayer and parked the tractor in the yard. I changed into some clean clothes, took dad's car and headed out east. The sun shone as I drove across Romney Marsh and the scene was idyllic. The marsh was at its best; the sheep stood out so plain, as newly shorn. Their new coats had not had the mud of winter to stain them; the crops were at their greenest, as was the grass. The heat of mid-summer had not yet cast its spell on them; turning the seeds ripe brown as it would do in the next four weeks. Sally's house stood proudly and forlornly out on the marsh long before I arrived at the gateway. The yard of the profitable arable farm of over a thousand acres of leased Crown land was very fertile, flat and well drained. The yield per acre put us to shame up on the hills, as this was a few years before artificial fertilisers came to the fore.

Sally's mother greeted me at the back door. Five foot ten inches, with permed hair, neat frock, clean, smiling face and a friendly manner, so unlike Mandy's mother. The yard was clean and tidy; the back door was newly painted and showed no wear. Rubber boots stood in an orderly fashion inside the porch, so unlike the house I visited earlier.

"Hello," said Sally's mother. "Are you looking for someone or selling something?"

"Well I don't know; perhaps, I'm not sure." Mrs. Wilton smiled,

"Come in young man. Looking for a job are you?"

"No, no," I said. "It's rather difficult to explain."

"Let me put the kettle on; we'll have a cup of tea shall we and you can explain what it is." Mrs. Wilton was so different from Mandy's mother. She had grace and manners and a smile in place of a scowl that would make a mad dog run miles to escape! The cups appeared from the Welsh dresser followed by a jug of milk from the fridge; then the teapot was warmed and a brew of Earl Grey was placed on the table. I felt like Royalty and yet she had no idea of who I was or much less the nature of my visit. I introduced myself. My father was an old friend of her husband's and she knew him very well.

"You must be John. They are always on about you running the farms with only two helpers. What brings you right out here today? Can I be of any help?"

"Well, our farm in Kent adjoins a farm and the other week I met their daughter Mandy." She interrupted me.

"The poor girl; her life is a shambles; the way they treat her. I feel so sorry for her. The poor girl is never allowed out; they will live to regret it. She will kick the traces one day and leave as soon as she can. She is so bright; and the way they abuse her. Sorry, you were saying? Only my daughter said that Mandy had met a young man on the adjoining farm, whose name was John and I guess it is you as Mandy is coming to stay this weekend and a John is calling for her. How rude of me, but those people do rile me so. Carry on."

"Well, I met the girl called Mandy and she asked me out, or I did the asking. She is staying the weekend here and I wondered if I would be allowed to take her out, as she tells me she is forbidden to see boys."

"Such nonsense! Of course you can; at her age she should be out meeting boys. We have a lovely daughter, Sally. Maybe you have met her? She has a boyfriend, a nice boy like you in many ways, polite and sensible. She goes out when she can, only it's not easy living like we do out here, but I suppose she will leave when she is eighteen or so to live in Ashford, or close by I hope. Of course you can take the girl out if you behave yourself with her, such a nice young girl, younger than Sally, but we must make sure that her mother doesn't find out. Have you met the mother? A right battleaxe and her husband, a right bastard! Sorry, I should not speak like that. My husband says it is nothing to do with us, but I think it is. Of course you know he's not Mandy's dad? That supposedly is someone else and that's why he hates her so."

"No, I never did; only met her mother today." I said.

"I'm sorry, I should keep my mouth shut, forget it, but please do come down on Saturday; Mandy is stopping all weekend, only it's our little secret. Another cup of tea and tell me all about yourself and the farm. I believe you have orchards. I love apples and cherries."

The afternoon sped by and a couple of hours soon went. Sally's mother could not stop talking and I was rather pleased to get away. I saw someone on a tractor pulling into the yard as I left and they waved a greeting at me. How different the two farms were. On the first farm the natives were very hostile, and this one so charming and friendly.

I drove home full of myself, it had been easy to pull the wool over the eyes of the wicked woman at Mandy's. That night Mandy was late; the moon was well up by the time she came the opposite way, for she had taken the longest route to see the new ride that I had made earlier in the day. She slung herself around my neck.

"Darling it is perfect; the going is softer up under the top hedge; his hooves make no noise at all and walking through the wheat is so out of this world. It sweeps down to the valley and is so gorgeous."

"Yes quite a view from up there in the day if the weather is fine," I said. We kissed and then I told her of my visit to Sally's home.

"You did what? I thought it bad enough when mum said you called on her this morning. You were lucky she was in a good mood." 'God, call that a good mood! I hope I never see her angry,' I thought to myself.

"Then you went to Sally's. What happened?"

"Nothing darling; it's all right, really it is. Our family know them; they are nice people."

"I know that, I told you that."

"Yes, well Sally's mum thinks it is a fab thing that I take you out. You should go out and meet people of your own age," she said. "Sally has a boyfriend and goes out."

"I know but she is going to ditch him next time she sees him and find someone like you who is not always after one thing. But I will never leave you or let another boy touch me ever again, I promise. Where are we going this Saturday? I can't wait!"

"All I have been thinking of my darling is that it has got to be somewhere neither of us is known, so it has to be far away from here. Mandy, leave it to me," I said. "We had better not see each other any more this week just in case your parents decide to check up on this new route. Come on darling, stop that and ride off home and by the way, what are your measurements?"

"My what?"

"Your size? "You must have nice clothes for Saturday and as you can't bring any from home …." She interrupted me

"I haven't got any at home; everything is second hand and worn out. I have never had new clothes."

"Well it's time you did; a girl of your age should have a wardrobe to dip into."

"Oh darling, you are so sweet; are you going to buy me something new? My dad said you are rich, always having new farm machinery and new cars. Can you bring that big new blue car your dad's got?"

"Maybe, but what are your measurements?"

"I don't know. I have never taken them. Tell you what; at school tomorrow, us girls will find out and I will leave a note here," and she touched the trunk of the old lime tree. "Please find it and buy me something." Then she ran crouched from under the low bough, vaulted like a cowboy on-to the back of her handsome piebald and galloped off into the night.

It was Friday before I found the letter pinned to the tree, left the night before by Mandy in exquisite copper plate handwriting. It read:

To my darling, from a 5'8, 34c cup, 26-inch waist, 32 hips, size 12. Love always, Mandy xxx

Saturday morning found me in town looking in shop windows at women's clothes; they were a complete mystery to me. I had never before entered a woman's clothes shop and slowly pushed the door open. There on dummies of plaster of Paris were all the things a lady wears. A woman shop assistant approached me and enquired.

"Can I be of any help as you look lost?" I showed her the note from Mandy and her face took on a smile. "Been given a birthday present list have we? Follow me sir," and she ascended the stairs into the upper part of the store where more mannequins stood, only this time clad just in underwear of all colours and shapes. I was dumbfounded; there were so many. The smiling woman introduced me to a girl of about twenty, and handed her my list.

"Elizabeth will help you," she said and left. I looked at the girl and she blushed.

"What do you wish to buy from the list?"

"The lot," I said. "It's for my girl."

"Ok sir, what colour hair has your girl? That will give me some idea of what will suit her, what does she usually wear?"

"A jumper and a blue skirt. Once she wore a pair of shorts and a silk neck halter."

"Oh dear, you have a problem. There is this," showing me a long dress called a pencil something or other. "That's a size 12." A garment in lovely black with white and red roses embroidered on it hung from a rack.

"Yes, that will do," I said.

"Or there is this," and she held a rail of garments open to reveal a red knee length skirt, "with this," she said, pointing to a white blouse. "That goes well."

"I'll take that as well then."

"Now the bra size; 34C. She's a big girl then," and opening a drawer slapped a couple of bras on the counter, one in black and the other in white.

"You are sure these are the right sizes aren't you?"

"That's what the girls said."

"Ok, but keep the receipts, just in case now. What about stockings?"

"There's no mention of stockings," I said.

"Well that's easy; they fit all sizes; she has got a suspender belt hasn't she?"

"I don't know; I haven't seen her in stockings," I said, "never found one," and I turned a deep red as I realised what I had said, 'never found one'. The assistant blushed as well and giggled; obviously I was one soft touch. I knew nothing about girls and was willing to buy anything she suggested.

So the items were wrapped and I paid sixteen pounds, three shillings and four pence, a small fortune. I left the shop with my bags and felt rather embarrassed walking down the street carrying the parcels from a women's shop, me, a young lad of the sixties. I covered the items up in the back of the car dad said I could have tonight. It was a new estate car with bench seats and a column gear change, a real passion wagon, all shiny and new. I was out to impress Mandy big time.

I spent half an hour in the bath that afternoon and put on clean clothes. I was away at five, arriving at the farm at six, having taken my time wondering about what Mrs. Wilton was going to say when she saw the presents I had in the back of the car for my sweetheart. I was met at the back door by three girls; Mandy, Sally and a girl I didn't know with long brown hair and a portly figure.

"Meet Judith," said Mandy, "and Sally." A blonde of seventeen with a perm, so unlike Mandy, was introduced to me. Sally had a tall frame with no shape, but to make up for all her feminine loss, she had a wonderful smile and manner and her voice was very cultured as if she had a plum in her mouth.

"This is Ox," Mandy announced to the whole house in her cheery voice. "Do come in," Sally said. "Make yourself at home." Sally's mother pushed her way through the girls.

"Let the poor lad get in." I handed Mrs. Wilton a large basket of fresh picked ripe Neapolitan cherries. "For me?" she said. "Thank you."

Mandy moved up beside me and looked into my face with approval. Today she wore a very washed out blue jumper and a pair of faded blue slacks whose legs were held tight by straps under her feet. The other girls wore the same sort of gear but stood out in new clothes.

"Where are you taking us girls tonight dear?" she said, and Sally's mother read the startled expression on my face, as I had not planned to take all three! I didn't even know there were three! "Don't be rude Mandy; a girl never asks. He said he would take you out, so he will."

It was obvious that Mrs. Wilton, although she knew Mandy should not meet boys, was only too willing to allow her out with a couple of chaperones.

"Now, let's have some tea," and I was shown into the sitting room with a large window that gave a panoramic view across ten miles of marsh to the distant hills of the North Downs, and a table laden with best china and plates of sandwiches and centre of place two massive homemade cakes. No way were we going to wade through this lot. Sally was thin and like a skeleton and Mandy was not a lot bigger. Mandy looked by her figure as if she watched her weight, but her shape lied to the amount she ate!

Then the back door was heard opening and Mrs. Wilton said,

"Ah, right on time," as her husband, a giant of a man, entered with his two sons. A glance at them, and the food told me that if we did not hurry up and grab a plate, little would remain.

The teapot made its appearance again for the second time, this time with real tea, and we all got to know one another. Mr. Wilton started to tell me of my father and when they had been in the scouts together and some of the things they did when young at camp and Jamborees. Then he asked where we were going for the night, as he did not relish Mandy's parents finding out. "Mandy's dad was a real bugger," he said "and Mandy's mother condoned it, but what, he would rather not elaborate on." Luckily Mandy did not hear what he thought of her father he would say no more. He liked the new car parked out the back and had thought of getting the same model himself. Then I remembered the clothes in the back and suggested that Mandy, who was next to me glowing with pride, she now had a boy friend, go and get the parcels and try them on.

"What are they?" she said.

"A gift for you, my love."

And again on the sound of those words, 'my love', she started to cry.

"You bought me something!" and the chairs scraped back across the stone tile floor as three girls pushed themselves from the table.

Sally said, "May we be excused?" and without waiting for an answer, was gone.

Jimper

Mandy was first to the car (just). The boot came up and the arms and hands were quickly in, grabbing the four parcels. They ran into the house with four presents and Mandy ripped the paper from the smallest to reveal to the audience two bras and a suspender belt. A hush came over all.

"Not here," I said, and Mrs. Wilton stood up and hustled the girls from the room. The men laughed.

"I say boy; you brought the weirdest gift. It used to be a box of chocolates in my days!" I explained in a funny sort of voice that Mandy had given me a list of things she had not got to wear and I bought the lot.

"Well, if you got the lot, I dread to think what the other bundles hold!" A shout from the top of the stairs said it all.

"It's gorgeous! Oh Ox; my love." Mandy was now using those words 'My love'. I turned a shade redder as the men in the room looked at me.

"Hit the nail on the head there young man!"

The shrieks of delight drifted down the stairs along the hall and into the living room while we poured another cup of tea. Then Mrs. Wilton entered the room and gave me a hug and kiss on my cheek.

"You have made that girl so happy. She claims they are the first things she has ever had new; only wants to keep the price tags on each item!"

"Price tags! Oh no!"

"Yes, my boy, you should always take the price tags off a gift to a woman. Never mind; she looks lovely. You will have to wait to see her; the girls are going to bath her first so the clothes stay clean. Mandy insists. Albert; you should see what he has got her. I have a mind to give you a list like the one in the dress parcel; it is all written in lovely old copper plate handwriting." I was unaware that the girl in the shop had enclosed the list with the garments as she packed them.

"Now my boy; where are you taking them tonight?"

"Canterbury, I thought 'no-one will know us there will they?'."

"Not in that dress they won't!" Mrs. Wilton chipped in.

A lot of girly sort of noise came to our ears as the girls dressed for the evening's event. At last Mrs. Wilton opened the door to a prearranged knock and Mandy stepped into the room. A sigh went up from us men; there was the most beautiful seventeen year old Kentish maid, dressed in a black slim pencil dress, covered in red and white roses, whose neckline plunged to her bosom and revealed a locket lent to her by Sally for the night. A dainty pair of Mrs. Wilton's sling backs that happened to fit like a glove showed from the hemline, six inches off the ground.

"Turn around Mandy; let them see," said Mrs. Wilton, and Mandy turned to show all her black lovely combed hair. I noticed that she wore no bra, but then her figure needed no support. One of the sons said, "With a little training, she could be a top model."

We all agreed; a most impressive woman stood before us.

"Ox, I can't accept this; it is so expensive and I have nowhere to show if off. If mum saw me, she would kill the both of us. This is for ladies, not me."

"Nonsense," said Mr. Wilton, "Don't you bother about your parents; no-one is going to tell them and Ox here has just the place for you tonight, away from all the eyes; and even I wouldn't recognise you the way you look."

The other two girls standing in the doorway appeared and started to go on about all the other things now strewn over a bed up in Sally's room.

"This," Mrs. Wilton said, "is the night the 'wicked' stepdaughter came of age."

Mandy swung round to face us.

"You've told them haven't you? You know don't you?" and she ran from the room in tears.

"Go John. Get her back. I didn't mean it like that; she is so pretty, I didn't mean it." I ran up the stairs, nearly catching Mandy up as she tried to leg it up the steps two at a time. In a very restricted skirt, she was having trouble. The shoes lay abandoned at the foot of the stairs. I grabbed her as she entered a white and pink wallpapered room and tried to hug her. She tore herself away from me, and threw herself on the bed on top of the new clothes lying there.

"I hate you!" she said. "You know about me. You did it out of pity."

"What?" I said. "What is it? What am I supposed to know?"

"You mean you don't know? They haven't told you?"

"No. What should I know?" And she rolled over on the bed to look at me. She grabbed me and buried my face in hers with her hands clean and soft like I had never seen them before and we kissed.

"I thought you knew; you are so kind."

"Now come on; stop crying and wipe those tears away," I said. At that moment Sally and Judith arrived and sent me downstairs.

Mrs. Wilton was so alarmed as she had no idea that what she had said would upset Mandy so. What was that secret of Mandy's? Mr. Wilton said everyone should know his thoughts on the subject, but his wife told him to keep his mouth shut. Maybe it was best kept secret. I was intrigued. Mandy was a mystery; the more I knew the girl, the less I understood but to find out more, I must tread very carefully if the performance I had just witnessed was anything to go by.

CHAPTER FOUR

The three girls appeared within half an hour. Mandy was still wearing her new dress but this time had on her new bra, her womanly stature proudly displayed, a girl of only seventeen, yet so mature. She was also wearing the pair of sling backs retrieved from the staircase, a little lipstick and a good dash of perfume. She looked sensational.

"That's better," Mrs. Wilton said. "Much more sensible for the type of place you are going to," and put her fingers along the top of her dress to tuck her bra out of sight. "Now behave you girls. Don't overdo it; it is very kind of John to take you. Now it's about time you went; I want you three in at twelve and no later, do you understand? Good luck young man; look after them won't you?"

We left and Mandy had a struggle to sit in the front seat. She had never before had a dress that restricted her legs and tried to pull it up, but the other two said,

"No, you get in like this; you sit first, then lift your legs together. " So Mandy was learning to become a lady.

We drove along the lane from the farm to turn left for Hythe, then onto the B2068, a twenty-mile run to Canterbury. The girls were impressed by my father's new car. It ran smooth and fast. The sun was warm and we entered the city in style, three lovely girls and myself. I felt proud. Mandy had never been to the place before; she had been nowhere it seemed. She went to school at Ashford but had seldom been on the streets. A bus collected them from the station and returned them in the evening to catch the train. Her mother was the only one apart from her big brother who left the farm. Poor girl; she so much wanted to look in the Cathedral and I promised that another time I would bring her for the day.

We found a good-looking hotel and parked up in the car park. The bar was not very busy and accepted non-residents, a four star hotel that had the elegance for my girls and unlikely to attract any one of Mandy's parents' friends. So we should be safe. A waiter greeted us and waited at the little table in front of us for our orders. I ordered three coca colas and as Mandy had already said that night in the moonlight, her drink was a cider. The drinks arrived and Mandy smelled her glass then drank the lot like a fish.

"Steady on," I said, as the other two looked on in amazement.

"It's not a race to get drunk; you are a lady now, not at home," said Sally. "Show some decorum."

And from that episode, Mandy changed as if a magic wand had been waved. From school she knew how the other girls charmed other people and behaved. So now she stopped from being the unwanted little country farm urchin. With new clothes, the first she had ever had, she changed for the better. Within months, she was to become a refined young lady who spoke with superb ease and elegance. Her whole manner altered away from her home and pony.

We passed the evening talking about everything that teenagers did in those early sixties. A wind of change was in the air; rock and roll was on the scene and it was agreed that I should find a venue for the coming weekend to take the girls dancing. Mandy was thrilled to think that she was going to live at last. Sally and Judith often went out on Saturday nights and were going to teach Mandy to dance in the coming week. Mandy and I cuddled up to each other on the sofa with my arm around her and every now and then I tweaked her bra strap through her dress and she gave a little titter.

"It feels funny wearing one of these," she said. "I wish I could wear it more often, only tomorrow I will have to go home and mother would want to know where I got it and from whom."

We left at ten twenty for the drive home. The sky was full of stars and the moon again shone down on us. The two girls were staying at Sally's for the night, even though Judith only lived a mile away. We pulled up in the yard and the girls said they would leave us alone for half an hour, then let Mandy in as the parents had gone to bed, for there were no lights on apart from the one in the porch. Mandy had only had three ciders in half-pint glasses, but they had the right effect on her. She was so happy in her actions and could not control her hands, or so she said! I learned the art of undoing a bra strap that night to a lot of sniggering from the girl who had never owned or worn one before in her life. It was hers to keep now and forever she told me, so I had to give it back to her, and as I loved it so much she would wear it for me when she could. The half hour flew by and I escorted her to the door, then embraced her tightly and said, "Goodnight, God bless, my darling." The door swallowed her and the light went out. I drove home thinking of the Moon Girl for every time we met, the old moon made an appearance.

I saw Mandy four times in the next week. She could not go to Sally's the following weekend, as her mother wanted her to work at home. There was a load of washing and housework to do. Her mother had been too busy in the week to do it. Slave labour sprung to my mind.

The following week our local hunt had a barbecue along with the adjoining hunt at a place called Westerham in Kent, near Sevenoaks. I had managed to get an invite. I had taken the liberty to ask Sally for her phone number while in Canterbury, so had some sort of contact through her to Mandy at school. Sally was seeing her boyfriend on the Saturday and said it was all right to collect Mandy from her home for the barbecue and let it slip that Mandy had nothing really warm to wear to a barbecue, but was sure I could find her something at the same shop in Ashford like last time. This Mandy was starting to cost me a lot of money!

On Tuesday I was at the pub having a quiet drink with Eric when Alan came in.

"John; how are you? How is the girl? Had a good night out the other night did you?" I was horrified. How did he know?

"Me? No, of course not."

"You should see your face," he said. "It's gone all red." I didn't know if he knew or was pulling my leg. If he knew, then how did he find out? I had to be careful. He sat down and we yarned about a house he was converting into a luxurious home. The old house had stood for years down by the river, deserted and falling apart. We often played in it as kids; it had a huge chimney that a chain and hook hung from and we used to climb up to the top. Now his dad had bought it and was going to make a tidy profit from it. At the moment it stood half finished and if I wished to entertain a certain girl, that was just the place if I kept it from anyone else. He was hinting that perhaps I could take Mandy there and I got the feeling that he knew more than was good for the both of us.

Mandy's safety was at stake, to say nothing of her character. Was it not him that had warned me only days after I first met her? I had known Alan for only two years and knew nothing of his family or where they came from. Somehow he held information that I thought I should know about, but he said nothing.

The following day was Wednesday and it was the local Rye market that Mandy's mother would be at, so I took myself to Ashford early, as I knew where she would be. The woman in the shop recognised me.

"Hello; here again?" She greeted me as I entered the shop for the second time in my life. "Have we a list again?"

"Not this time," I answered, "but I know what I want," and climbed the stairs to Elizabeth's floor.

"Remember me?" I said.

"Yes of course. Was everything all right?"

"Marvellous," I said. "Now I wish for something to go to a barbecue."

"I've just the thing for you. Wait here," and she vanished to another part of the floor to produce a skirt of knee length, made of brown pleated moleskin, so smooth, waist perfect.

"Would sir like a top to go with it?"

"I think so. She will look silly with nothing above it!" She smiled and bent down to pull a drawer open under the counter to produce a jumper of green lambs wool. "That goes well." She spoke in a low voice as a lady customer had now entered and stood waiting her turn to be served. Another older girl came over from another counter and engaged the woman; they kept glancing my way and tittered. I was the subject of the day. A young lad in a female's domain! Not the done thing in the elderly customers' generation.

Elizabeth enquired whether my young lady had a slip to go under the jumper; I told her that I had no idea, so a silk garment was added to the growing pile. Elizabeth asked if I would like the three garments gift-wrapped and I jumped at the opportunity. The cash till rang and I was poorer by eight pounds and seven shillings. I walked down the street, more confident this time than the previous time, my shopping hidden in lovely gift paper. On my way home I stopped at Brookland Post Office and addressed the two parcels care of 'Miss Sally Wilton, Land Farm, Romney Marsh, Hythe.' The man behind the counter weighed the parcels, took my money and placed stamps on the packets.

"Get there tomorrow morning," he said, cancelling the stamps with a rubber ink marker and tossing them into the sack hanging from a peg behind him marked 'local'. So Mandy should have them on Friday night when she came home with Sally from school. I left the shop, feeling happy that it had gone so well, then the sky opened up and the rain came down, bouncing off the road as each droplet collided with the surface of the water, trying to drain off. It really was a deluge. I prayed it would not carry on into the weekend and spoil the party for the evening, but by the time I got home half an hour later, the sun had came out to play and the sky looked a lot lighter.

Friday found me out in the middle of the marsh on our farm chasing sheep into a pen and shearing off their fleeces. The day was very warm and the forecast was for more of the same tomorrow. I packed the wool away for the day and went to the pub to see if I could find Alan as being Friday he should be there in the darts team. Sure enough there he was.

"How's it going then?" he greeted me. "Not courting tonight then?"

"Courting only old sheep" I said. "Been shearing all day, can't you tell. I stink, even now after a bath. The oil from the fleeces gets in the pores of your skin, makes all your skin soft."

His turn came up and I scored for the game, which he lost, so we sat at a table. He had a pint of bitter while I had my favourite tipple, a Coca Cola. I am a teetotaller. I have tried almost every alcoholic beverage and never found one I liked, so stick to soft drinks. I was careful of what I said to Alan but along the way I found out his family had lived in Kent for over a hundred years and originally came from Gravesend in North Kent, but I was no nearer finding out how he knew of mine and Mandy's nocturnal whereabouts.

The following day father said I could stop work as soon as I had cut the five acres of clover that we had for hay, so I rose at seven am, mounted the tractor at eight and set to twenty minutes later. After an hour of mowing I picked up an old pushbike frame that some idiot had cast into the field six weeks earlier and which had been covered by the grass. The chatter of the slipping clutch told me something was amiss I stopped immediately and lifted the blade from the crop. The damage was done; two mower fingers missing, two bent to buggery and six blades gone. Two hours of swearing and sweat had the cutter working again. I did not finish until three pm and had a bath. Then in father's car, ready with a full tank of four-star petrol, I set out to meet darling Mandy.

The sun was hot, just the weather to turn green clover into good hay and even better for a barbecue. I entered the private road up to the farm and saw Sally and Mandy come out of the front door to meet me. I never noticed what Sally was wearing as the sight of Mandy took my breath away. There she stood, looking so sexy in her new skirt and light green jumper, a real lady, as if her father was a lord and she his favourite daughter. I pulled up and she flung her arms around me.

"Oh Ox! I have never had a parcel through the post before; now I have had two with my name on them. Look. Do you like it?" She twirled around to display the pleats in her skirt that showed off her well-formed legs to perfection. The stockings of sheer nylon caught the sun and only stopped when they ran out to reveal a suspender button and naked leg.

"I love you darling," Sally said. "Steady on; mother may see!"

"I don't care," said Mandy. "I love him."

The sensation of owning new clothes was going to the young girl's head. Surely she does not know what love really is, the way she behaved that first night we met, and the way they treated her at home. We kissed and returned to the house where Mrs. Wilton greeted me.

"John; how sweet of you to send the skirt and pullover by post. Mandy was so thrilled she cried with joy. I very nearly opened one when they arrived, then at the last moment caught sight of 'Care of Sally' written on the parcel. She jumped with joy to find the pullover, then when I gave her the other one, she cried. Such a lovely skirt; I wish my husband gave me things like that, and such a surprise, you even thought of a slip! It's for tonight I suppose because there was no note that we could find, so presumed it was from you. Now have some tea before you go; it's four thirty now and it is over an hour to Westerham. I don't expect you will be back very early," and a young man walked into the house through the back door.

"Martin. How are you?"

"Hello, Mrs. Wilton. Very well thank you."

"John, do you know Martin, Sally's boyfriend?" and a five foot ten blonde haired lad shook my hand.

"How do; pleased to meet you." I had to wonder, was he the one that Mandy said Sally was going to ditch, or a new one I had heard nothing about.

"Watch yourself with her John, be careful; her parents are rough, if you know what I mean aren't they Mrs. Wilton?"

"Yes my son and it would be advisable to not talk to people of it. Walls have ears you know."

Martin was a carpenter and worked in the local town and had known Sally from an early age. We four sat down and had a little tea; then at five thirty we left for the barbecue. Martin and Sally sat in the back and Mandy took the seat alongside me, taking her place like a lady. No more was she the little country urchin in old clothes; She was now one up. She was a girl of means. With new clothes, new car, good pals with manners, and educated speech. That day Mandy changed. Her schooling had been buried with her family; now she could be the lady she wished. Within minutes the conversation led to her new clothes and how proud she was of them.

For the first time in her life she wore new, bought for her, and the manufacturers had got the size right. She let slip that the only things not new tonight were her shoes and something else. We had by this time reached the town of Ashford, and I noticed at the same time she said, 'shoes', a shop that sold the items, and pulled in.

"Right; I'm not having my girl wear someone else's shoes any more, so out and come on hurry, it's nearly closing time." Sally and Martin were the first out.

"I can't." said Mandy in her shy timid voice. "You have spent too much on me already and I will never be able to repay you."

"I don't want money, only you happy," I said, "now come on, quick."

Sally grabbed Mandy by the hand and pulled her up as she remembered to swing her pretty legs out first.

"Come on Mandy, hurry up!" and you said there was something else?"

"Not now," they whispered to each other as Martin and I shut the doors.

"Ox. Got a pound note on you?" said Sally. "There's something I need now," and as I handed it over, she said. "See you in a jiff."

Sally vanished off along the street, only to reappear ten minutes later as all the shoes that two girls were producing from cardboard boxes were swamping Mandy. In Sally's hand was a brown paper bag.

"Here's the change," she said, offering me four shillings and two pennies.

"What's in the bag?" I said,

"Don't let him see; it's a surprise for later, from me to him", said Mandy and the two girls giggled and Sally stuffed them in her handbag.

"Now hurry up; these people want to go home' it's nearly six," I said.

"Those," said Mandy picking a pair of brown shoes up that had a strap across the top of her foot, with a little button to hold it firm. "They are lovely. I'll have those thank you."

The woman took them away as the girls rapidly shoved the pile of shoes back into the boxes, ready to go home. I as usual paid; three pounds, nineteen shillings and eleven pence. So madam was now shod in new shoes, which came out of the parcel the moment we were all in the car and on our way again, the little brown bag forgotten about for a while.

Then on reaching Tonbridge, Mandy and Sally wanted the public loo by the station so I had to stop. Martin and I lit up a cigarette and had a smoke as the girls made themselves scarce, reappearing a few minutes later. Mandy deposited the brown bag into a litterbin with something in it.

"What did you throw away in that bag?" Martin asked Sally as she again took her place in the back.

"Women's things," she said. And we left on the Sevenoaks part of the journey.

CHAPTER FIVE

We started to see signs for the barbecue long before we got there. We could make out the other people who were going and it became a sort of game to guess who was who. We drove into a large field, and I mean large. It was huge, at least forty acres, packed with cars. Some barbecue this was going to be! All the knobs were there but Mandy was just as good as them and a lot smarter than many. Her long black hair shone in the evening sunlight and you could pick her out from a long way off. We had been there only a few minutes when I met Mr, Finch with a couple that I knew and they said,

"Fancy you turning up here! Old Piper is here. Let's find him and his daughter shall we?" My heart sank for although I knew Mr. Finch, he did not know Mandy or her friend Sally. Mr. Piper I knew was acquainted with Mandy's dad as he farmed the opposite bank to us and being a big corn grower, more than likely knew Sally and her family pretty well. This was a bad idea to come here. We four made our apologies and crept away to hold a 'Council of War'. All agreed for Mandy's sake that tonight was off, or at least here. A rapid evacuation was made; the open road seemed safer from prying eyes. "Where to?" said Martin.

"No idea," I said. "Let's find a pub."

Mandy was more than pleased with this suggestion so we went in search of a public house far from home where we could perhaps let our hair down a bit. We had not long to wait when a large pub appeared with a big car park half full of cars, and it was only eight o clock. Outside was a lovely garden where you could take your drinks so we made our way there and I went to order a beer for Martin, two cokes and a half pint of cider for the delectable Mandy. The sun was warm; the air was still, a real June evening. Slowly the pub filled up and the sun sank in the west. As the evening progressed, the folk in the garden left. We sat and talked of everything but mainly about the top ten records of the day.

Martin bought the second round and the evening was going with a swing. The light was fading from the sky when Mandy gave a scream and clasped the side of her right shoulder.

"Whatever is the matter?" we all chorused together.

"A wasp has stung me and I am allergic to them."

"Hell," I said, "Now what?" Mandy started to shiver and sweat and had a job to get her breath. Sally ran to the bar.

"Call an ambulance quick! A wasp has stung my mate. Help!" A man stood up and declared that Sally must not panic. He was a doctor and would see what he could do. The woman with him left to get his case from the car. The doctor followed Sally to the garden that was lit by coloured lights.

"All right, my dear. What's your name?" "Mandy Smith", she said.

"Ok now, keep quiet, it's all right."

His wife arrived with the doctor's case; she told us to stand back and give the girl some air and she took Mandy's jumper off to reveal her new bra and slip. The wound was under her right arm and only just visible. The woman examined her green jumper and found a wasp on the outside.

"You are lucky it's a thick sweater my love." The words 'My Love' were not responded to as when Mrs. Wilton or I spoke them. "The wasp has only just managed to touch you." The doctor gave Mandy a pill to suck and said she was not going into shock. She was more frightened of the sting than what damage it had done, but he was rather concerned about the bruising on her left side and the marks on her shoulders. What had she been doing?

"Nothing," she had said.

He asked how old she was, and if she worked. As if it had some bearing on what he detected of her body. She told him she was seventeen, and still at school. Mandy put her sweater back on and the doctor and his wife left for the bar. We calmed down. That was a close call. If Mandy had ended up in hospital, her parents would have been told. Tonight we had escaped.

Mandy said she wanted another drink and could she have a brandy for her shock? We all agreed that maybe that was best so I went to get the drinks, two brandies, as Sally said, Mandy's scream had also given her a shock. Martin had a bitter and me, the old coke. While I was waiting to be served, the doctor sidled up to me and told me.

"Be more careful with your girlfriend; treat her with more respect; you obviously don't know your own strength."

I informed him I always treated her with the utmost respect for she was precious. He said,

"Maybe, but if you carry on the way you are, she will get hurt and I don't wish to see her injured. Take it more carefully."

I paid for the drinks and left the bar, never to see that doctor again. I pondered on his remarks 'to treat her with more respect'. Who, me? What was he on about?

The full moon shone from a clear sky and Mandy felt better. She sipped her brandy and loved it. She was sorry for the fuss she had caused, only her little brother had nearly died last year from a wasp sting and she believed it ran in families. She had never been stung before and it hurt. I said. "Let me look," and she let me peep under her jumper. A small red mark was the only thing visible. "That's OK," I said, with confidence and we carried on chatting, "We had better get on home," I said.

They rang last orders in the pub so we all left; Martin and Sally arm in arm, Mandy and I much more slowly, as I pulled her closer to me and walked the short distance to the gate. As Sally and Martin disappeared around the corner, I turned Mandy to face me and we kissed, her embrace and kiss so soft and loving.

"I love you," she said, "for caring for me and thank you for the shoes and clothes," and she gave a little step to show off her brown leather shoes to me.

"Come on," called Sally. "Plenty of time later for that."

We walked to the car. The trip home in the moonlight took forty minutes. We slowly drove into the yard with our headlights off and parked around the back of one of the huge corn sheds. Sally had suggested the idea that we had an hour each to ourselves and Mandy and I left them in the car to walk in the moonlight. Twenty yards further on we turned the corner of the barn and spotted the shed of straw.

"Beat you to it," she said, and her new shoes started to earn their keep. She was faster than me this time, unlike the first time. We crashed into the straw and I hugged her. Then we sank into the loose straw around the bales. The night was warm; the hour quickly passed by. Then Sally called us.

"Coming!" I said,

We went to find Sally and Martin. I knew Mandy's appearance was only straw and drink but she was still the same girl I had bought the shoes for. We had been good and I had been very careful of her as the doctor had said, but his words, the words of a medical man, worried me. Did I hug Mandy too hard? She had never told me to be more careful, only 'don't mark her'. Was there something I did not know of girls? The doctor had asked how old she was, and if she worked as if they had some bearing on her injuries. I was not going to tell Mandy that she alone was the first girl I had ever had or kissed and as I was nineteen and lived on the marsh like Sally, isolated from girls, I knew little of sex apart from the bare facts. My mum and dad never touched each other while I was around and I never read books so girls were a mystery, apart from Mandy, to me. Now I had been warned by a doctor to be more careful. I needed advice.

I kissed Mandy goodnight as Sally did Martin, on the doorstep and we two boys left. Mandy had said she would meet me on Wednesday under the lime tree, so I dropped Martin off in town and drove home to muse over the day and especially what that doctor had said. Everyone was telling me to be careful of Mandy. What was the problem? I had to know and now.

The following day, Sunday, I had to find Alan at all costs and try to find out more of Mandy and what made her tick. I had a good idea where he lived and got the house right first time. His father came to the door and invited me in. Alan appeared down the stairs looking rather bleary eyed, even at eleven o clock in the morning, obviously a late night last night, or a very heavy one. "Alan, we need to talk, my friend," I said. "This Mandy."

There was a clatter out in the other room that turned out to be the kitchen where his mother was preparing the family dinner. She came in through the door like a tornado.

"Did you say Mandy? Not that Smith girl? You don't know her do you my boy?"

The expression on Alan's face told me to say nothing.

"Mandy Smith? No, Sherwood from Rye. Who's Smith?"

"Oh, that's all right; never you mind," said his mother. "Only that name is taboo in this house if it's Smith. Now sorry, excuse me. I dropped the roasting tray," and she vanished back into the kitchen from where she had come. Alan then relaxed.

"Thanks," he said in a hushed voice. "Only don't speak here. I'll meet you at the Bell at twelve. See you later."

He turned to open the door to show me out. This was really getting interesting! Now even Mandy's name made a grown woman drop the dinner. Something was amiss with my lass and I needed to know.

The pub was open. I ordered a cheese roll and a coffee for a change. Alan arrived ten minutes past twelve.

"Right Alan, I need to know all there is you know of Mandy."

"I can't tell you anything," he said. "It's more than my life is worth I promise you. Keep away from her," and he turned on his heels and left.

"Alan, don't be like that; I must know.'

"Now look John. You don't want to know. Just keep away and don't bother my parents."

He got in his car and drove away; I had upset him big time by just saying Mandy's name in front of his parents. I had to find out what the big mystery was. Sally's family was my only hope but I did not want to spoil the relationship I had with the family as they allowed Mandy and I to see each other. Perhaps it was more to do with Alan's family. I would ask Sally when I could get her on my own. Now how to do that? The station. She came home on the train to Hamstreet? How did she get to her home from there? I would have to see her somehow with out Mandy knowing.

So next day at four thirty I lay in wait for the train from Ashford to arrive, hoping Sally would get off before someone came to met her. There was no sign of a car to pick her up. As the train pulled into the platform, I hid out of sight in case Mandy was on the train my side and saw me waiting for she would want to know the reason for me to be so far from home. I had no reason to be waiting for this train that was now delivering a load of school kids on the platform. Sally got off with a friend and hurried outside into the road as a bus pulled up. "Shit; a bus!"

So the method of her getting home was solved. I ran to the car and followed the bus at a distance. As it kept stopping, I had to overtake; I reasoned it would take Sally to Hythe and to stop being observed by the driver overtaking, and then letting him overtake me, I went to the next turn off from the marsh lane that Sally lived up. Soon the bus appeared and took the road to town. Sally was looking out of the window, saw me and waved. Now I had to see her if only to explain what I was doing in her road. I followed a few minutes later then the bus stopped and Sally got off. I tooted my horn as the vehicle drove away. She was with another girl and they were both pleased to see me.

"What are you doing out here today John? Sally said.

"I need to speak to you alone," the girl with her said, "Is this the one you call The Ox? I see why!" and smiled at me. "I'm Lucy."

"Nice to meet you," I said, offering her my hand, which she took and shook.

"Must go Sally; see you in the morning."

"Sally," I said, "I really must talk to you about Mandy".

"Not now," she said, "I have a hair appointment. Give me three quarters of an hour." So I sat in the car as she had a new perm put in her hair. I opened the door of the car for Sally to sit as she came level with me.

"How are you?" she said. "Good night Saturday; thank you for taking us. It was a pity about the wasp sting, rather spoilt it for you and Mandy."

"So long as she is all right," I said.

"Oh yes; her usual self, full of you and the new clothes you keep buying her. Can't stop her at school."

"Right," I said. "What is the matter with her? Please tell me the truth. Why must I be so careful with her? Whatever is the matter?"

"Nothing as far as I know only she's madly in love with you. She's very strong, so I don't know. Why? Did you have some concern?"

"Well yes. Everyone says I must be careful with her."

"No, not her! Her parents you silly boy; if they ever find out…" and Sally held my hand, "I hate to think what they would do. They are strange. If they find out about you two, her life will be terrible; they are so possessive of their eldest daughter." Sally then gave me a kiss on the cheek. "I'm sure that is all it is. Now are you going to give me a lift home Ox? I love that name for you. Mandy is clever the way she gives people names."

"I know Mandy is clever because she is studying for law."

"Yes, I cannot understand her; it is so difficult; the teachers love her for doing it."

Sally took my other hand and patted it. "Now don't worry; there is nothing wrong with Mandy. She will go to university you know, but why law?"

"Beats me." I said, "To get her father's inheritance or something."

"Oh I expected it was something about her father and the way he was cut out of the will for marrying Mandy's mum. You do know about that don't you?"

"Yes, she was a gypsy wasn't she?"

"Well not a gypsy, a Romany; there is a difference you know. The Romanies are a very loyal crowd; you don't upset them! They are lovely people if you leave them to their own devices, but upset one of them, and you upset the whole tribe. Poor old Mandy; she even looks like a gypsy with those eyes and her long black hair; she is the envy of the school."

"So you know no reason why I must be careful other than her parents?"

"No, nothing, and she will not talk of them even to her friends."

I thanked her and dropped her off at her door telling her that her hair looked fabulous. Giving a wave to her mother as she gathered the washing from the line I drove home.

Wednesday night and the full moon again shone on the land turning everything into stark relief against the skyline. The shape of fields a mile away stood out in the moonlight. I sat under a thorn top near the old lime tree so I could see the landscape lying out before me. The air was full of nightingale song that nested around the wood in the brambles and undergrowth. I heard Mandy's approach tonight, three fields away as she sang to David, his heavy breathing portraying the haste she had made him do, carrying her from the farm to me over one mile away. They came to a stop and I grabbed his bridle as Mandy slipped off his back.

"Darling I have missed you." She showed how much by the way she put her arms around my neck and smothered me with her lips and hair, that she had the habit of throwing around me, pressing her body to me in a suggestive manner. I stood mesmerised holding the bridle of the pony.

"Let me tie him up for you."

"No, let me do it; I know how to."

She flipped the loose reins over the top rail of the gate near where we stood. "Look at that view tonight," she said, "So light; I even saw the badgers out in the field on my way down here. They take no notice of me on David at night."

We lay over the gate with our arms around each other and I was happy just to do so, but Mandy wanted more so we lay on the grass in the moonlight and petted. My hand caressed her soft warm body.

"You are so slow," she said as we kissed goodnight. "You will never see your present from me at this speed; you do know you could have had me tonight my darling don't you?"

"I don't mind." I said, kissed her again and squeezed her harder.

"Mandy behave yourself; you are only seventeen; don't spoil it."

"I love you," she said, gathering David's reins up; she pulled her body onto David's back and trotted away up the hedge and I thought to myself 'that word love was becoming her favourite word'.

"Goodnight, take care," she sang out.

"And you," I said. "God bless, see you tomorrow." Then I got wondering what her present was that she'd had now for four nights that I was too slow to see.

Life was good and I lay over the gate and dreamed, 'If only I was not so worried of getting her pregnant, I could be having the time of my life but I reasoned that could wait for now; being careful of Mandy worried me more. What did others know that I did not? Even the doctor who did not know her saw the reason. It must be medical and I was frightened to ask Mandy to her face in case she did not know. Surely that was the reason no one talked of it.

Alan knew and was scared I would tell Mandy, as she did not know herself; perhaps she could die suddenly if something happened to her body. She had been scared of that wasp sting. Yes it must be something like that I thought. How could I see her again in the daylight? Where could we go?

The invitation to use the house that Alan was doing up came into my mind but the opportunity never came up as Alan's father sold the place that week. Soon we would be busy with the harvest then the corn would come first. Courting would have to take a back seat for a while. Then the winter weather was on the way and as we did everything out under the stars, it was going to get cold.

I decided as Mandy was going to be at Sally's again this weekend, I would take her to the Cathedral in Canterbury. A new set of clothes, perhaps, especially if the girl was so ill and could die if not careful. So I walked back up to the yard and drove home to my bed.

Next night I met Mandy but we only had twenty minutes to ourselves as David had gone lame; she'd had to run to see me and could not be long. She was supposed to be in the shed, which she used for a stable where the pony was confined, and if her dad, mother or brother found her absent, the girl would have a lot of explaining to do. I told her of the plan to go out on Saturday and we agreed to meet at nine am. We kissed the best we could, as she was breathless. I told her to walk back, not run, and sing aloud to herself so her parents could hear and realise she was on her own and not bothered about being found. Mandy had a wonderful melodious voice, so strong yet so clear and dreamy; she could charm the birds from the woods and put the nightingales to shame. I heard her sing as she crossed from the gill into the home paddock singing 'Jamaica Farewell'. Her voice floated across the still warm air to my ears. We both were so happy.

I went home and next day presented myself in front of Elizabeth in now 'my shop'.

"Hi; how are you? Come for more clothes for the lady?"

"Well I really need something that is special. My girl has an illness and could die any minute." I had now convinced myself that this was the only reason for the 'be careful' bit of advice.

"What is your girl's name?" "It is so rude to keep saying 'her'.

"It's Mandy." "That's a nice name young man; she is lucky to find you. Now where are you thinking of going as it may help to dress Mandy if it is a special occasion. I know her size; twelve isn't it? And very long jet black hair."

"Forty four inches." I said.

"Gosh! I imagine she looks gorgeous." I could not have described her more aptly I thought. "Now let's see what have we got? Where are you going?"

"To see Canterbury Cathedral," I said.

"That is a lovely church; it's where the Black Prince is buried. His tomb is inside. Now you want something like this I suppose. How tall is she?"

"Five feet eight inches," I told Elizabeth.

"Just the thing," She held out a knee length skirt, and a white blouse to go with the black skirt. "Something of this kind sir, off the shoulder with big lapels, with short sleeves. It is a good match. Now anything else?"

"No, that will do nicely."

"I'll wrap them for you sir."

I paid and walked the familiar way back to the car park, pleased that Mandy was an easy shape to dress. It had taken less than thirty minutes to accomplish this mission. 'Canterbury look out! Here we come!' I thought as I crossed the railway bridge and took the road to Rye.

The rest of the day I was lumping hay bales on and off trailers for in those days it was all pitch forks, long before big bales and hydraulics. The hay was taken to the barn and unloaded by hand, to be stacked inside, a nice lot of clover hay for the sheep come January.

CHAPTER SIX

Saturday dawned clear and bright. Mother knew by now that I had a girl and insisted that I had a clean handkerchief in my pocket. A new deerstalker hat from Dunn's in Hastings, which matched my tweed jacket and highly polished brown brogue shoes. She stated that I would do and I left full of confidence to meet Mandy. A fast drive across the marsh brought me to the farm. Mrs. Wilton greeted me in the garden.

"What have you got their young man," noticing the packages under my arm, "not more clothes for that girl? The girls are up but I am afraid that Sally has got to work until five tonight so will be unable to come with you. She is upset because she says that you are such fun and a real gentleman, but I see no reason why Mandy and you should not enjoy yourselves. Sally can go another day I'm sure." My heart lifted higher. Mandy on my own all day! I relaxed. "Go in; they are in the kitchen."

No they weren't as I found out on approaching the door. Mandy and Sally were coming out to meet me. The girls had seen the parcels under my arm. Mandy gave me a little kiss and retrieved the packages from my hold at the same time, saying.

"This for me? You shouldn't," the girls disappeared in side untying the string and unwrapped them in three seconds.

"Darling," and she slung her arms around my neck. "They are lovely; let me try them on," then vanished behind Sally up the stairs. Mrs. Wilton had come into the room and stood observing the scene before her, putting an arm on my shoulder said. "Cup of tea John? If nothing more, you have made the poor girl very happy again, and that's what she wants right now. It is a very difficult time for her right now. Do be kind to her; don't do anything stupid."

"Mrs. Wilton…"

"Call me Shirley," she said, "Sounds less formal and we do know each other. I thought of talking to your mother the other day. I saw her in Rye but she was busy. Does your mother know you come here?"

"Oh yes, and that I have a girl."

"That's nice; I will tell your mother about Mandy; so nice and clever you know. Sits her exams soon for University to study Law. I'm sure she will get into Oxford or Cambridge." She got two cups out and placed them on the table, "Mandy has such a head on her shoulders, and she will get away from that family. Have you met the family?"

"Only her father and her mum the other week she looked fierce to me."

"Fierce! They are a law unto themselves. We once had over twenty down here."

At that moment the kettle started to boil so Shirley made the tea.

"The threats if we had the police. Going to burn us out and we were frightened I can tell you. Here have a cup of tea."

A cup of Earl Grey was slid across the table and Mandy then appeared at the door.

"My God!" Shirley gasped. Look at her!"

Bare feet and legs to the knee, then a black skirt made for her, to a white blouse, tanned arms and neck to a princess of perfection face. Her dark eyes shone like ambers, surrounded by black hair that hung down her shoulders to her waist at the back.

"Mrs. Wilton! Look what he has got me. Don't you love him? You must not keep bringing me such expensive clothes darling."

"Don't be silly Mandy; it gives him pleasure to dress his love well and anyway you will need things that are nice at college."

"I'm not going to college; I want to stay with John."

"Don't be silly Mandy; you are going to make something of yourself, to escape your parents." Mandy swung around, her hair making a wide ark with the movement and ran upstairs crying.

"Oh no, not more waterworks," I said.

Mrs. Wilton left the room and closed the door. I heard Sally's voice raised in anger as they talked to Mandy then the back door opened and Sally's brother came in.

"Hello," he said. I recognised him as the tractor driver and the one who ate all the food at the tea the other day. "Mike how's it all going?"

"You must be after Mandy she's here somewhere," he said looking around the room, not knowing I knew the girls were up stairs.

"John I have heard a lot of you from Alan." Alan! The name hit like a sledgehammer.

"You know Alan?"

"Yes; we play cricket together. He's our No. 4 bat. Damn good he is. I told him you were down here the other day with the girls, taking them out."

The reason Alan knew of my darling Mandy's actions was clear; it had nothing to do with the warning. What was I getting worried over? His pleads of not saying were all a tease; he knew nothing, only that where I was from Mike. Mrs. Wilton appeared.

"Michael; your lunch is in the box and your flask is made. See you at six."

"OK Mum," he said picking an old army rucksack up from the back of a chair and left, "See you around more often, we are playing in Rye tomorrow, see you there maybe."

"Perhaps," I said." I logged that in my brain Alan would be there; maybe I could apologise for the encounter last Sunday in the pub when he left in a hurry. Sally then appeared with Mandy; she stepped up to me and put her arms around my neck and buried her head on my shoulder.

"I am sorry Ox," She tiptoed to kiss me. " I do want to go to University, but I don't want to lose you."

"I'm not going anywhere my dear," she sort of slid from my body and walked around me to Shirley.

"You are right; he is a steady lad," and she put her hand out to hold mine. "I don't deserve him do I?" Mrs. Wilton came over and put her arms around both of us.

"Come on now; you are fine. Now go on out and enjoy yourselves."

Mandy had the road map spread out on her lap as I drove to the city, 'just to make sure,' she said, that we were going the right way, even though I knew the way and had driven it three weeks before, with no help! All the signposts pointed 'This way' for Canterbury. We found a place to park and walked arm in arm along the streets, with the Cathedral dominating the skyline ahead of us. Mandy kept stopping to look in all the shops; she had never had the chance before.

She was like a child in many ways. A shoe shop appeared and a glance at her feet showed me she was in need of new footwear having only a pair of old white plimsolls on her feet. I asked her where the new shoes that I had got her were," she said Sally had told her they were not the kind to be seen walking around town in the daytime, she looked down at her feet. My eyes followed hers.

"Those darling are casual shoes" I said, "Now today we are a step up from casual in here," and held the large glass door open for her. She walked in with a sideward look at me.

"What are we doing in here?" she said.

"Take a guess. It's time my lady had another pair of new shoes to go around town with, the pretty likes of you my love should have a choice of footwear for every occasion." Oh God, those words again! Please don't, not in here I prayed and the tear in her eye stayed in the corner of those dark eyes. I gave thanks to the Big Fellow up above that this time Mandy had not burst into floods of tears.

"Pick whatever you want," I said. She started to look at all the latest fashions. A rather nice pair of black two-inch heeled ones caught my eye.

"What about these?" I said, pointing to the pair. And she picked one up. "Heels?" she said. "Me on these!" A woman came up to us.

"Can I be of any help Madam?" Mandy looked at me and silently mouthed, 'Madam!' was the woman talking to her!

"Yes," I said. " The lady likes these; have you them in her size?"

"Certainly sir. Take a seat madam." And pulled out a stool for Mandy to sit on rapidly pulling her old plimsolls off to show her perfect toes. The assistant arrived with an arm full of boxes. I stood back as the woman put shoe after shoe on Mandy's feet. 'This was going to take all day,' I thought, as the two started to chat like girls do.

"This the first time you have had heels my love? Sensible to start with two; four is too much. Some girls over do it but they don't have confidence, better start short. There they are lovely, now this pair your size, the same as those," and she lifted the top off the box to reveal a pair in cherry red. Mandy's eyes sparkled.

"Yes, those." That was it. She looked stunning. Red and black were her colours. As a girl wrapped the old pair of dirty plimsolls up, I popped a tin of cherry blossom shoe polish in the bag.

"Must have that," I said. "Bet she hasn't got red at home." The woman looked at me and said.

"Doubt if there is any kind of home, Sir" taking another look at the pair of plimsolls she had wrapped. I tendered eight pounds for the shoes and polish, and got two pence change. Mandy was now two inches taller and it showed. She now rose up in the world. Her face was alongside mine and she kissed me on the cheek.

"Thank you darling; wait till Sally sets eyes on them." She lifted a foot out in front of herself to show them off.

"Sally said you would buy me a new pair when you saw the plimsolls. If you go on like this you will have to buy me a house to put it all in."

"Some hope, I said. University for you my girl," We laughed… I walked as she tottered alongside.

"It's weird," she said, "but I will get used to them." We entered the Cathedral and spent over two hours inside. Then we went to find food, as we were both getting hungry. Together we found a French restaurant and sat at a table, Mandy read the menu of over eight courses. If only a country urchin and not allowed out, she was well versed in food and French. She had little else to do at home so read and had a very intensive brain. Once seen she never forgot; a good start for a lawyer. We both had roast lamb followed by a pudding. I paid and we left to window shop. That was a joke; we only glanced at the windows then entered. I carried the bags that increased in number with every shop we visited. Mandy had nothing so every item was new to her. The first thing was a set of handkerchiefs with her initials embroidered in the corner. With a smile I paid. Next was perfume. How she hoped to explain to her mum, I had to know.

"I will tell her that Sally had it as a present and does not like it, so she gave it to me." The third shop was a jeweller's, an expensive one this time, she yearned to enter and look at the crucifixes. She had always wanted one but her parents forbade it. Religion was not allowed in her home although a lot of her close family was buried in a churchyard. Mandy secretly prayed to God as she 'believed', and had been taught at the little school when she was young, it was only since they had moved to Kent that religion had been denied her. I asked her if she was baptised.

"No of course not. Mum does not allow it, but I hope to be one day."

She found a small cross on a gold chain for her neck and I paid for it. She insisted I place it around her neck and she kissed the cross. She would wear it at school and keep it in her bag when she went home each day. Then as we were making our way back to the car, Mandy spotted an ice cream parlour that had two huge Knickerbocker glories displayed in the window.

"Ice cream," she squealed, "please!" So ice cream it was. It arrived with a cherry on top and a long spoon that stood proudly out of the cream level with her eyes. The girl looked at me and put a hand round the glass. "All mine!" She said in a soft voice as if to acclaim that she would not share. My banana split arrived as Mandy shovelled the cream into her mouth, prodding and poking with her spoon to see what delights lay hidden under the next layer of ice cream, a lady's refined manners having a period off! A child yes, a few precious moments for Mandy as in her child hood she had never been allowed such treats. The delight on her face made up for all the drips running down the side of the glass. That mess cleared away, I paid and we left arm in arm. Happy now after all that time in church and window shopping, less of the window, plain shopping in my mind by the amount of bags in my left hand, with my right arm around the girl I loved.

Walking with confidence and already suggesting that two more inches would be lovely and did I know she was shoe size six. I made a mental note to add that to the dress and bra size list at home.

It was four o'clock when we left the city, and as Sally was 'working at the trains' as Mandy put it, 'plenty of time to take another route home to meet her', and so armed with her map, I followed Mandy's instructions and at a place called Barham. A lane looked inviting so as it led west, we turned down it to take us home. A mile along the hedge bound lane, the verge under some old elm tree's opened out, and had been occupied by some Romanies' caravans, all painted in fantastic colours. Their ponies grazed the grass and the dogs were tied to the wheels of the wagons. Kids abounded and all their grubby faces turned to see who dared to pass along their lane.

"Stop," said Mandy, "my people."

Her people? Lord, how did she know this lot? But she didn't. She had meant it's her blood. A shout from one of the older men as Mandy stepped out in her red shoes with her long black hair brought over eight women like her from the vans. They walked down the four or five steps from their respective doors and hugged my girl. I was spellbound! Did she know them? They seemed like long lost friends, but in reality they were her relations as the true gypsies came from Egypt hundreds of years ago and have their traditions and funny ways that, as Mandy later told me, 'was born in you and could never be forgotten.' I got out, leaving the car in the middle of the road.

"Come over," One of the men said.

"How did you find us? Where do you come from? What camp you from gal? What's your name?" and she said,

"Mandy, of Elgin Smith."

"My girl! You the gal of Tiger of Essex? Gal of Martha and Elgin Smith of Billericay?

And a chatter of voices ran around the group of women in a funny language. "They be looking for you the last four years."

This was news to me, I knew nothing of her relations; Mandy would not discuss it with me.

"You now be old enough now my girl."

"I know I am, but I am not one of you really," She showed them her crucifix that she had got that afternoon.

They hugged her. "Never mind; you are one of us; come let's celebrate."

"No," said Mandy. "We must go. I will see you some time again soon."

I opened the car door for her and took a last look at so many girls and women not unlike my Mandy. Long black hair, eyes so piercing, and brown tanned, golden ringed fingers, all the same.

"That Ox, is my true blood; we are all related somewhere down the line," she said, making her self comfortable again in the seat "but I wish I had not told them who mum was. They will be after us now they know the place we live."

"They don't know where you live," I said.

"They know the area now," she said. "They won't rest till thy find me now."

And she started to cry

"Dad will kill me if he finds out; don't tell him ever, will you?"

"No, of course not. I seldom see him." Mandy laid her head on my shoulder and sobbed. "I must tell you but I can't, Oh' darling I do truly love you, you do know that don't you." She cried even more and her whole body was shaking. I had to stop and take her in my arms, "darling what is it?".

"John" A name she seldom called me," I can not tell you here lets go home please."

Back at Sally's all the shopping bags were transferred up to Sally's room and when Sally arrived home, we three went to Sally's bedroom to show Sally today's haul. It was like Christmas! The shoes were the talking point for five minutes and Mrs. Wilton was called upstairs to see them. The cross was next, to be followed by the tin of polish, even that got a mention. Then a red deep v-neck off the shoulder blouse that I somehow had let Mandy buy for herself with my money in one of the clothes shops. The first item she had ever picked out and exchanged for real cash. Then the perfume, three pairs of socks, and to go with the shoes; a pair of fishnet stockings that Mrs. Wilton thought were rather 'not Mandy,' but the girls loved them. While all this was going on, I had noticed a large five-year diary with a lock and clasp in brass on the bedside table.

"That's nice," I said. "Yours Sally? I keep a diary every day; have done since 1952."

"No," Sally said, "that's Mandy's. Top secret; won't even let me look at it, or the likes of you."

Mandy flew at me as I picked it up. "Leave that alone you are never to see what is in that, have you got that," and the manner of her voice, I had never heard that tone of voice from her before, and every one there realised she meant it.

"It's all about her boyfriend and the presents she gets." Said Sally, "Only joking John, but she says its full of her secrets and no-one is to look."

"Fair enough," I said, "the same with mine." The significance of that diary meant nothing to me then but later it would come flooding back. Mrs. Wilton said, "They were all lovely presents

Jimper

and tea was ready for whoever wanted any, and Martin would be around at seven to go out."

I followed Shirley downstairs leaving the girls to go once again over today. Mrs. Wilton told me, "Not to spoil Mandy as the poor girl had to go home tomorrow and live with her parents. It was not easy to leave a carefree home like this for what she is going through; please take special care of her and don't hurt her more than I need to." I asked her what she meant, how was I hurting her, just be easy on her she said. I was going to have to look that word care up in my Funk and Wagnall dictionary when I got home. It seemed I did not know quite what it meant. It must have more than one meaning.

With tea out of the way we washed up. Martin had arrived in the meantime; we were going dancing in Folkestone at the Lees to a real band tonight. Mandy appeared in her red shoes and black skirt, only this time she had her new red shoulder-less blouse on, along with her cross and perfume. Wow! She had done her hair with care and it shone like polished coal. Talk about a dazzler! She was tops. Mrs. Wilton took a look and said, "She was too young to dress like tha,t and again, "take care of her."

We left for the channel port with the sun behind us. Mandy kept close to me all night, when we were not rock 'n' rolling. She had stamina. Her feet moved like lightening. Her whole body vibrated a sexy tune. The other boys there could not keep their eyes off her and she said she felt threatened when not holding me. Sally and Martin were engaging themselves vigorously to the music as they were used to the rock scene. Poor Mandy was a learner but had been taught well by her mates at school in the last three weeks.

Too soon it was time to head home; we took the road under the cliff and joined the main road at the bottom of the hill at Sandgate. Soon we pulled into the yard behind the barn. The house was in darkness apart from the porch lamp. The old moon was out and cast little light tonight through the layer of cloud but Mandy and I knew the way to the straw shed. We were soon all over each other but we behaved ourselves, although tonight I found her surprise from the week before. A little red pair and she said Sally had got her a pair of white ones at the same time with my pound. I tucked the red pair in my pocket telling her she had lost her knickers forever. They were mine now, but perhaps the postman could sort something out for her. She was so soft and warm. I explored her body that night trying to find out anything that the doctor had found, but I found no lumps that were not supposed to be where they were. I tried to bring the subject, of what she had to tell me, but each time she buried my face under hers and kissed me moving her body around on top of me, it was as if she did not wish me to know, and she wanted to forget.

Then Martin called our names and we had to go. We had talked tonight; she told me that she truly loved me, but was frightened her parents would not let her go away to university, and would I come with her if she did go? We could be so happy; there would be no need for me to ever look at another woman again, she promised; she was trained to make her man happy. I did not know her meaning of 'trained to', although if tonight was any thing to go by, there was only the act of full intercourse to complete our love, I was so sure Mandy could satisfy all my wants. The trained bit of the conversation made me wonder what she meant. We stood on the back door step unwilling to part but the night was fast moving to day.

The drive home was a void in my life that night, as I tried to make sense of the day past. There was some thing my darling Mandy wished me to know, but could not tell me herself, more of the gypsy theme I presumed so put it out my mind.

Soon we were to start harvesting and apple picking. To see her would be hard and as she said, school holidays started soon, then she could not get to Sally's. Her parents would not run her down there and they would not pay for a train or bus. She wished she could have a job to earn money. But her parents forbade it. That night we had arranged that I would put a fertiliser sack on a bit of string and hang it along the road from hers in the holly tree on our farm so that she could see it from her bedroom window. That would mean that tonight I would be at the lime until eleven pm. She was thrilled. What an idea. No one will know of our own signal. We had kissed so persistently on that doorstep that I hoped she had not hugged me too hard and hurt herself. The moon shone on the bonnet of the car all the way home that night. I filled my diary in and placed my little trophy between the pages and thought of Mandy writing her diary up. Little did I know the significance of that locked book of hers? I then had an idea. Mandy had mentioned her family did not go in for religion, but now she had a cross to wear around her neck while away from her home.

She had said that one day she wanted to be baptized, and by the manner of her voice when she told me made it evident that to be christened would make her happy, and that was uppermost in my mind for I felt very attached to the girl. To make her smile and be happy was the number one thing. She would not need her parents' consent to be baptised in church she only needed to take a Christian name to make it legal, so surnames need never be mentioned and her family need never know. So nothing was stopping her; she only needed two Godfathers and a Godmother, a font with water and a willing vicar. It was so different from a wedding. I reasoned that babies never chose their Godparents so why should Mandy? I surely could arrange two men and a woman for the day to fill the required gap?

Mrs. Wilton was the woman that sprang to mind immediately. Yes I would talk to her; she was a responsible person. If she thought it a good idea, perhaps I could arrange it as a surprise for my girl.

CHAPTER SEVEN

I visited Land Farm one evening knowing that Sally was at violin lessons and didn't get home until seven thirty. Mrs. Wilton listened as I explained my concerns over Mandy not being christened.

"Yes, a lovely idea, but I should ask Mandy," she said, "and if the answer was yes, we could turn the event into a special sort of day and have a party at lunch time. She was confident that her vicar at the local church in Lydd would be only too pleased to add another one to the flock. Of course, because of Mandy's age, she would need something special to wear, but now I had thought of that hadn't I? With the skill I had in choosing her clothes to accompany me out. "An off white at her age," she said, "would be most appropriate. When was I to see her next?"

"Tomorrow night," I said. Mrs.Wilton was surprised and turned to look at me.

"How do you see her at night?" she asked.

"Up on the farm," I said, "when she is riding around in the moonlight." Shirley smiled. That's why you call her your Moon Girl is it? Sally sometimes called Mandy 'Moonlight girl'; now I know the secret. Be careful my lad; don't get caught. The family is a rough old lot, but you know that. Mandy must have told you of them."

"No," I said; she hardly ever says a word of them; only tells me to watch her dad and mum as they are evil."

"Maybe she is telling you the truth; I hope not," and left it at that. I was still no wiser of Mandy's family and friends, if any."

"Let's have a pot of tea shall we?" She said. "Sally will be back in a while."

At that very moment a car drew up in the yard, and Mr. Wilton and Sally walked in a few seconds later.

"What are you here for John?" She said as her face lit up on seeing me. To a young person, any young face out in this desolate area was a welcome sight.

"He's here to see me my girl," her mother said, "not you."

Sally looked disappointed and dropped her bag of schoolbooks in the corner and went up to her room. Mrs. Wilton busied herself getting the tea things out, at the same time running the talk we had just had by her husband.

"A splendid idea," he said, "but I don't see why Sally should not know." A head then stuck itself around the door.

"Know what?" She had been eavesdropping outside I guessed.

"Mandy getting her hair wet and a party." It seemed too good to be true. "She would have to have all that hair washed if she was to present her head to a vicar. That would take all day!" she exclaimed, "but I could help her. Go on John ask her. She has talked a lot of religion since that visit to the cathedral in Canterbury. Go on; arrange it mum, please! I know that Mandy will be thrilled."

"No Sally, wait. John is going to ask Mandy first; it's only right he does. But I will see the Reverend tomorrow and see what it involves."

I had tea with the family and left at nine pm, a very happy boy. Next night could not come fast enough and as I waited up in the cherry orchard I heard her voice not far away. David and Mandy were on form and appeared in haste and she jumped from his back into my outstretched arms.

"What is it you want to ask me? Sally said it could not wait at school today. She was bursting to tell me. What is it my love? Tell me, please tell me!"

"Mandy; you remember you said you were not Baptised the other day? Well, would you like to be?"

Her body stiffened and she swept her hair from her face with both hands, letting go of David's reins in one movement.

"Can I do that?" she said.

"Of course, if that's what you want," I said.

She grabbed the hanging headgear before the pony realised its mistress had let them drop.

"Oh darling. I love you! When? How? Where?" She gasped, all in one breath, and let her whole body's weight lay on me. "A real Christian," she sighed at last. "I can say my prayers without feeling guilty of asking Him to do things. I will belong to Him and His church. I always feel He does not listen to me as I am not baptised."

"Don't be silly. He listens to everyone, no matter who they are my sweetheart," and we kissed. "How is David, has he made a full recovery"?

"Dad says he is fine but I don't think he is a hundred percent. When do you think I can see the vicar?

"Don't worry over that, it is being sorted out."

"Please Darling, try to get me christened." She said in her excitement as we kissed goodbye for the night. "I hope he hears me, I so pray he does, I so want it to stop."

Mandy was not making sense, and when I asked what she wanted to stop she told me to forget it. I was relieved that my idea was greeted with such enthusiasm, but what did she want to stop?

Sally's mum phoned me that following night. Sally had told her that I had seen Mandy and it was all systems go. Mrs. Wilton had seen the vicar and he had suggested the Sunday week, following Morning Communion, also that it would be nice if I attended as I was confirmed, and maybe took the young girl to the altar for a blessing while we all received the Holy Sacrament. If I agreed the date was OK, she would go ahead and arrange a large lunch for afterwards with perhaps a few friends from the village as well to welcome Mandy to the fold. She was as thrilled as if her daughter Sally was getting married and to have been asked by me to be one of the Godparents as was her husband. Martin, Sally's boyfriend was also ecstatic at the idea that he should be asked to round the three Godparents off. Mrs. Wilton had taken it upon herself to ask the vicar if he knew of a church person like himself to be another Godfather she thought that as Mandy was nearly eighteen and been church less all her life, maybe a religious man could help her with any questions she had. He had suggested his brother, another vicar, now retired but very active and sprightly for his age; he knew his brother would be overcome with pride to be asked. She asked if I had any idea for Mandy on the clothes front, I said that perhaps she would like to come with me to choose something. She was speechless with excitement at the prospect. "If I really did not mind, she would be delighted." So over the phone that night it was arranged that I would pick her up the next morning at ten.

So the following day, I picked Mrs. Wilton up and drove to Ashford. We parked and walked to the large shop. We both went upstairs to see my personal friend, Elizabeth.

"Hello," she said, "brought your mother today?" and Mrs. Wilton looked at me in an old fashioned way.

"You do come here a lot lately don't you? Have you always brought your girl's clothes here?"

"No never." I said. "Mandy is my first girlfriend," I confided to her. Elizabeth came round our side of the counter.

"What are you looking for if I may ask?" Mrs. Wilton took over from here. "He is after a dress for the Baptism of an eighteen year old girl." My face went a shade redder. It was easier on my own with Elizabeth. Shirley was making me embarrassed.

"Let's have a look over here," she said, " is it your girl with all that black hair."

Mrs. Wilton gave me a more meaningful look this girl even knows Mandy's hair colour, she led the way through into a section of the store I had never seen before, full of wedding and bridesmaid dresses.

"Something cream," said the girl, Mrs. Wilton had spied a white wedding dress on a mannequin in the centre of the floor.

"A dress made for a bride. Just the thing," she said, "she was as pure as a bride and it was the only sure thing she would do once in her whole life." Shirley was stroking the gown as if it were a cat. "You can get married as many times as you can find the man, but to be baptised in the Church of England, you can only do that once; it's for life." I turned the price tag around and read thirty guineas. I mouthed the price, 'thirty guineas!' And swallowed hard I only had forty pounds on me, a small amount of wealth for 1960, and a massive fortune for a dress, I thought to myself.

"That is in size twelve," said Elizabeth, and Mrs. Wilton looked again at me.

"How many clothes have you bought Mandy John? She even knows the girl's size!"

"A good memory," I said.

"I do hope so," she said. "You surely cannot afford to shop in these luxurious places too often! If you can afford to buy that for Mandy, I will buy her a pair of white shoes to go with it. Then she will be like a princess." I had one other item to buy for Mandy but Mrs. Wilton was getting in my way; it would have to wait until I was on my own.

The dress was packed in fine tissue paper, placed in a hard cardboard box and tied up with string. I paid as Mrs. Wilton looked on with a smile on her face, pleased to be with me on such an auspicious occasion. We left and proceeded to a fashionable shoe shop and bought a pair of white slipper type shoes with low heels. Although the dress would meet the ground, she would have to wear stockings so Mrs. Wilton left me alone and went into another shop to purchase them. I took the opportunity of being on my own to I made one more visit to a shop in town, this time to a bookshop where I bought a white Prayer book for three pounds, with a gold embossed cross on the cover for Mandy to carry on the day, and in the future to use in church, I hoped.

On getting back to the Farm, Sally was there dying to see the dress, but her mother would not allow her to look; nor at the other things we had bought as they were for Mandy the surprise was to be absolute for the following weekend when Mandy was expected.

Yes Sally could tell her tomorrow at school that I had got her something to wear on the day but that was all.

The next ten days dragged by, and I had time to go shopping for the gift that I had been too embarrassed to purchase in front of Mrs. Wilton. I knew of a shop in Rye opposite the town hall that sold such garments, here on an upstairs floor I found the ideal thing in a small box, in three different colours, a selection of twelve knickers. The woman said nothing, took the money, and I fled. I wrapped the little box up in brown paper and sent it to Land Farm, care of Mrs. Wilton. I was not going to let my love go naked because I now had her red ones in my diary.

I saw Mandy three times in the evenings under the old lime tree but would tell her nothing about the day coming, or the parcel's awaiting her at the farm. She said she hoped it was not white as that was for her wedding and as much as she loved red, it had better not be too bright. The last time I saw Mandy was on the Tuesday before the church affair I arranged to meet her on the Saturday for a fitting, just in case anything was the wrong size. Then I had time to get it changed she had said. I wondered what Sally had told her and wondered to myself what she was expecting.

That Saturday I made my presence known at Land Farm at ten to ten. Mandy had not slept well, as until I arrived they had not been allowed to open the four parcels that sat in the front room like Christmas presents awaiting Christmas morning. As soon as I entered the house, Mandy grabbed me and flung her arms around me.

"My love. Come with me," before I could wipe my shoes on the doormat, I was dragged by the excited girls to the room for the opening ceremony. Mandy grabbed the largest box and undid the string. The lid was taken from her hand by Sally and she unfolded the tissue paper and held up her new dress, she did not bother to wipe the hair back from her face were it had cascaded in her hurry to lift it from the box, the water works where unleashed. No matter it was pure white that was forgotten by the sheer beauty of the garment, she stood holding the satin dress out in front of her perfect body and cried. The last was the packet of white stockings and everything was shipped up to the bedroom for a fitting.

Half an hour later the two girls appeared, still in their normal clothes and Mandy was still crying. She hugged me and told me that it was the most marvellous thing anyone could have given her; Sally had agreed that I must wait until tomorrow to see her in it as they both thought it would be bad luck. The Bible was another matter she held it close to her chest saying that I must write a message and date it inside, to Mandy with love and sign it. She read that wonderful book from cover to cover many times I was later to hear. The little box the postman had delivered in the week was handed to her on Friday night as she came home from school, and on opening it Sally had said that is all there was. I wished to see her at the church with only them on.

That night I left early, as I was to take the girls to the Morning Service at ten am. Mandy appeared in the doorway at nine forty looking like a queen ready for her coronation, a red rose pinned to her dress. Mandy was being baptised today and she was making a statement that this was no ordinary little girl; she was Mandy! As we entered the church, a whisper went around the congregation and heads turned. I took Mandy and Sally by their arms, and sat at the front. People who did not know of the event thought I was the groom, Mandy the bride and Sally the bridesmaid, so unreal. We all three went to the altar rail and Sally and I took bread. Mandy did as told and knelt with her head bowed, clutching her new Bible and received the blessing. A tear was evident from the little droplet that splashed the highly polished oak rail she knelt at. Her now washed hair from the night before hung like a black veil over her upper body.

The vicar announced at the end of the service that the girl was going to be baptised into the Church of our Lord and anyone wishing to stay may do so. Out of forty souls present that morning at eleven fifteen, only about half a dozen declined the invitation and we all crowded around the font as Mandy was baptised, having met her old and definitely not so sprightly Godfather, she managed to control her feelings and not cry. Then afterwards she took the new 'Father' of hers by his arm. Slowly the two walked to the centre of the rail, knelt facing the altar and both prayed. We could only stand and watch. My thoughts dried up with emotion. This was my little dirty gypsy girl with hardly any clothes and riding a pony, now dressed in real fine clothes, praying with an old vicar less than six months later. All the people knew the Wiltons and left with them. Sally went with her dad, and left me behind to drive Mandy and her new elderly godfather the half-mile home when they were ready. The atmosphere was like a wedding.

Laughter and joy filled the house as Mandy and I entered the house with her new father. A real party was held and went on into the evening. Over thirty local people had somehow managed to crowd into Land Farm that day and the thought struck me that out of all these people, someone would talk about the marvellous day and Mandy's parents would get to hear, as I was sure not all knew the secret of the Christening.

The evening party went on until one am and I think Mandy was too occupied with all the goings on to think about crying, and she told me that she was already thinking of getting confirmed, thanks to her elderly Godfather. He had seen a chance to get another into the flock before he popped his cassock, and to make sure he was still with us tonight one had to keep giving him a prod, the late hour and many glasses of wine were evident. Mandy was again in tears as I left her that night. She wanted to thank me for the pleasure I had given her today and all the gifts. The dress, she said, was going to be packed away for her wedding and she hoped I would see her at the altar in it, a subtle hint of the things to come I thought.

The following week the weather was good and the barley was coming off well. By Friday we were well ahead with the harvest and dad decided, as the forecast was for more fine weather, all the men could have the weekend off. I made tracks the following day and climbed the holly tree in the hedge that stood thirty feet high. From the top I rigged a ring of iron to a bough through which ran a line of bailer twine. I did not fancy the climb too often the leaves had thorns that tore your flesh. Then from the ground I hauled my flag to the top. That evening at seven I was encamped under the old lime tree waiting for a vision. Alas she did not show and I prayed her family had not got wind of the baptism, so at half past eleven, I went home, stopping on route to lower the flag.

Sunday I was at Lydd to watch a cricket match as I had missed the game in Rye when Sally's brother was playing, but our local paper told all that the last match of the season was to take place today. I had to see Alan and say sorry. Perhaps he only knew what Sally's brother told him. He was there all padded up, ready to take his place, which was not long coming. Eighty four runs and number three was caught out, so Alan strode across the pitch tapping his bat at the ground as if to see it was still hard after the dry summer we had experienced this year. He was run out on one hundred thirteen, unlucky for him. His team went on to lose by three runs; a hard fought season came to a close. He had acknowledged me as he was batting so I went and found him in the pavilion. He spoke to me as if nothing had happened.

"How are things then? Still seeing that girl you silly sod?"

"It's all right," I said, "I know how you get your information. Through Mike, Sally's brother," and he slapped me on the back.

"Sorry," he said, "but I couldn't help it. The expressions on your face each time I mentioned her name, but for God's, sake do be careful!"

There's that 'careful' word again I thought it just will, not go away. "Come on Alan; what do I have to be careful about? Mandy and I have never made love and anyway we would use something. I don't want her pregnant."

"No you fool! I don't care about that; it's her parents you must watch out for." I don't know why, only mum and dad keep on to each other about Mandy and her mother. After your visit up home they had a blazing row over what mum thinks, and dad not letting her say any thing about it. Something is wrong, take my word for it." We moved away from a chap that had entered the pavilion and was looking for some one by the way he was moving his head from side to side. "How did it go the other day then?" I did not know which day he was on about, so told him of the day out in Canterbury, and how on the way home we had met some gypsies and Mandy alleged they were relations.

"What? Real ones in those old horse drawn caravans? Where? My dad goes on about them. He says when he was a boy they used to come to the village, all the mums and dads kept their kids indoors until they had gone. They used to steal kids you know. Cor! Wish I could see them. Where were they?"

"Over at Barham," I said, "only about twenty miles away."

"Come on John; I'm finished here now. Let's have a run out. Your car or mine?"

"Mine I think said Alan; I have only had a pint; got to drown the old season; somehow won nothing this year. Lousy wickets and bowlers, no good, too dry, you know."

The lad of eighteen spoke like an old pro. As his car had more petrol than mine we decided to leave mine parked up and took his car, unknowingly this was to cause him no end of grief. He took the wheel and half an hour later turned into the lane from the west. Along the way we came across a pony grazing and Alan said, "It's a pity about Mandy's pony wasn't it?"

"What?" I said, "going lame?"

"No; having to have it put down."

My heart sank; her love and joy gone and I did not know.

"Yer; her dad shot it. She told Sally the other day; didn't you know? Don't you ring Sally to find out the news?"

"There they are," Alan said as we rounded the corner. A little girl was playing with her doll in the middle of the road so we stopped, to be immediately surrounded by gypsies. I got out and said.

"Hello again," a broad smile came over the old man's face that stood before me.

"My boy," slapping me harder on my back than Alan had done earlier.

"Come, bring your friend. Have tea."

We went over to where a group of them were sitting on lumps of wood and got into verse with them. They wanted to know everything about us and would tell us little of themselves; they wanted to know all there was of the girl I had been with the other day. They knew her father and he had never seen her. I looked up at him.

"Her father lives with her and her mother."

"No my boy; that's not his child; he is Lord Mc'Inty's son; the gal's mother got that gal from Jeremiah. It's his gal so be careful. Now do you know where she is?"

Alan looked at me and touched me on the arm. "Time we went," he said,

That horrid word 'careful' came flooding to my mind.

"You're not one of ours," the old man said looking me all over. "Work outside though do you. "Now where's this gal. She yours is she."

"No, I was just giving her a lift."

"I see," he said, "and that your car?"

"Come on," Alan said,' and he was already on his feet." Sorry," he said. And we ran to the car.

Luckily the little girl had moved as we sped off with twenty gypsies now standing in the lane looking at us speed off.

"He said be careful of that girl John. My parents keep on about them. I knew something was wrong with her."

"Shut up about your bloody parents, will you?" I said.

"She's not his daughter."

"I know that, it's who this Jeremiah is."

"Sounds like a gyppo to me."

"Of course he is," I said, and he's never seen Mandy."

"Could mean trouble," Alan said.

"Could?" I responded as we turned out of the lane onto the road to Lydd.

"Tis trouble John and we are in the bloody middle! I did warn you," Alan said "and you took no notice, did you? Been taking advantage of the poor girl I expect, and that will not go down well with them."

"No, I have not. How dare you say that; she's still a virgin as far as I know."

"Oh well; it's trouble anyway. I don't want anything to do with it."

CHAPTER EIGHT

Alan dropped me off at the cricket ground to get my own car and I came home and looked up Mr. Wilton's number in the book. No one answered so I supposed they were out; then the phone rang and I picked it up.

"John? Thank God it's you. We've got to talk quickly."

It was the number four batsman from earlier and in a hell of a panic by the sound of his voice

"What?" I said.

"A bloody gyppo followed me home from Lydd; must have got us mixed up; thinks I'm you. Came and knocked on our door, now mums on the case, your names mud, just wait till my parents catch up with you, and then you are for it make yourself scarce and Pub in three hours don't be late!"

I was at the door of the Bell Inn Iden before the iron bolts banged back to announce the pub open for the evening session. Alan pulled into the car park as I ordered.

"Make that a pint of bitter as well," I said to Gerry, the publican, and took my coke to a table, as Alan came in.

"Ah John, thank God you are here! What are we to do? They know where I live and it's all your fault, mum and dad are going up the wall."

"My fault? How do you work that out? You were the one who wanted to see them this afternoon."

"Yes, but it's you they want."

"No it's not; it's Mandy you idiot. She is the one they are after."

"I told you to be careful John. What are we to do?" His pint vanishing down his throat in record time.

"Another please," I said to Gerry whom had been listening with interest to our conversation. "If you don't mind for my friend." "And we my friend, like it or not, have got to sort this out once and for all, now spill what do you know Alan?"

"Nothing; I have told you. It's my parents; they are the ones that keep on arguing about something to do with Mandy."

"Right; what do they say?"

"Only that I'm not to have anything to do with her since my brother sat by her on the train home from school, that's all."

"Hardly seems a hanging offence to me; there's more to it than that."

"Of course there is, but what?"

"The gypsies want their girl back and you said your dad says that they used to steal kids. What if Mandy's parents stole Mandy from the gypsies?"

"Yer; that makes sense but Mandy knows she is of gypsy blood."

"Yes but maybe the story of him being a lord's son is a lie and he is a son of a gyppo; there is no lord or sir. They say that to make it look good."

"Of course, I bet it's her dad they want; he killed someone or stole something and they want to find him. That's why Mandy's mum is boss. You never see him out on his own; it's always her. She protects him."

"So Mandy is safe?"

"Of course she is. It's 1961 boy; no one goes around torturing people or duelling with pistols at dawn any more!" I stopped in mid speech, as the door opened and two rough looking men came into the bar.

"Christ, it's them!" said Alan. "The one I was telling you about who followed me."

"You idiot; he's still on your tail and now you have brought him here with a mate. What are we going to do?"

"Too late," I said, as one sat at our table.

"Day to you," he said, "nice day." His mate bought two Guinness's over and joined us. "Ok; which one of you came to the camp with that girl?"

I had to tell them; no way was I going to deny that I knew the girl. I loved her; but I was never going to betray her. If they wanted to know of her parents' whereabouts, I was not going to be the one to tell them. We got talking about things in general but I was on my guard for any trap. They asked if the girl rode at all and Alan could not keep his mouth shut.

"Not now she doesn't. Her father shot her pony ten days ago." The two gyppos turned to face him.

"So you know the girl very well?"

"No; it's him; she's his girl." Pointing at me. 'Thanks Alan I thought.'

"Why did her dad kill her pony?" the older one asked, looking at me now.

"I don't know," I said. "It had a bad leg."

"Did she ride often then?"

"All the time, around the farm." Damn, I thought now they know they have a farm.

"So they have a farm, do they?"

"No, not theirs; someone else's, where she works." I thought I had covered my tracks with that comment.

"Poor lass losing a pony; hope she soon gets another one."

"No hope," I said, "they can't afford it."

"Don't be silly," he said, "she must have a pony. You in here every night? the unshaven one said to Alan, "here tomorrow night, And the girl's name is Mandy right?"

They got up and left in an old truck. We watched out of the window.

"Funny," said Alan; "I thought we were in for a hiding there. Another coke John?"

"Yes please."

"Bloody hell; what do they want tomorrow?" he said as he waited for Gerry to come through from the snug next door.

"Don't know," I said, "but should be interesting to find out."

He changed the subject to other things, along with Terry who had come in. We thought it better not to tell the others of our visitors. We left at ten thirty pm, Alan and I made sure there were no strangers around to follow us.

The following night I did not finish combining until turned seven. On entering the back door at home, mother said I had better get up to The Bell fast. Alan wanted to see me Now! She said he sounded none too pleased with what he'd got.

I left immediately, still covered in dust from the dry crop wondering what he had got tonight as a surprise, not another visitor I hoped. On turning into the car park I saw Alan jumping around the yard on the end of a bit of rope attached to a large piebald pony.

"Thank God you have come! Look what I have been given for 'Your Mandy.' Now take this," and he gave me the rope. "All yours," he said. "I want no part of this! I've been here for over an hour with this bloody thing."

I was left with a very anxious pony and by the look of it, completely unbroken. My worry was what to do with it now. The problem of how to give it to Mandy would have to wait. I had to find a home for this boisterous pony tonight. I had a friend who was the local vet and his wife had horses, so I tied the pony up to the nearby fence and went into the pub to use their phone. The vet's wife answered the phone.

"Hello John; you want my husband or a vet?"

"No, neither; you."

"Me? Steady on boy; what can I do for you?"

"It's rather tricky; I have here a pony that is looking for a home for a night or two. I wonder?"

"OK; where are you?" "Up the Bell inn," I said.

"Right; give me twenty minutes and I will be with you with the box."

I put the phone down, thanked Gerry and went to see the pony and wait for Mary. I opened the door and instantly saw the pony was gone. I rushed to the bar; Alan was sipping the beer I said I would pay for.

"Alan! It's gone!"

"What has?"

"The bloody pony! It's missing!"

"Good," he said. "It's wild!"

"We have to find it," I said.

"Where did it go?"

"I don't know," "I left it tied to the fence and it's snapped its rope halter."

"It can't be far," he said and the mate of ours Terry who had joined him to find out what the horse was for said.

"Well let's go; perhaps the gypsies stole it; they were about earlier."

"Don't be daft," Alan said. "They bought it here for John."

"Him?" he said, looking at me. "What? Going into gymkhanas are you?"

"Come on," I said. "Mary, the vet's wife will be here for it in a moment." Out in the road it could have gone four ways as the pub stands at a crossroads. A pushbike loomed into view. Mr. Ball was heading for his customary pint.

"Have you seen a pony on the road?" I asked.

"No lad."

"Right," I said; "that only leaves three ways and there are three of us; come on Alan. You go to the Peace and Plenty and into grove lane the other end. If you find it on the way, stop and drive it back this way," pointing to the lane, "I'll go with you and turn right and go along to Cold Harbour Lane. Terry, you stay here and stop any car that comes and enquire if they have seen it, and ask Mary to wait for us."

Ten minutes later we were all back in the car park, to be met by a smiling Mary with her land rover and horse box trailer, which was now occupied by an animal trying to kick the side out.

"Hello John," ignoring Alan who was now starting to get worried at the loss of the pony.

"It's a fine beast. I came into the car park and saw it in the next door's garden drinking out of their fishpond. No trouble at all, so quiet; led it down the path, walked straight into the box, but I think it hates men. Saw Terry and went ape." With that comment Terry threw his hands in the air, turned and went into the pub. "Now listen to him; he can hear your voices. I think he's been hit by a man, they don't forget you know. Where did you get him? He's a lovely Pinto."

"A what?" I said.

"A Pinto, the type of breed. Did he cost a lot of money? They are expensive you know; and what's his name?"

"Alan; what's his name?"

"Don't know," he said. "They just said give this to the girl, 'Mandy' gave me the rope, gave the horse a good whack on its arse and left."

Mary looked lost.

"I don't want to know," she said. "It's getting dark. You could call him Kicker; he's doing a lot of that."

So Kicker left for his new lodgings, leaving me with the problem of how to unite him with Mandy. I could not just walk up to the door with a pony and say, 'For you girl! Present from me.' We returned to the bar where the knowledge of Mandy and me was now well established, thanks to Terry and his big mouth. The only way they could see was to take the animal up to Mandy's farm in the middle of the night and dump it, when daylight came they would find it. There it was, and no one would call to collect it so it was there's, but I pointed out how would Mandy know it was hers? And she would never feel safe with it not knowing that at any moment the real owner could show up. No, they had to know it was a replacement for David.

We left the pub without solving the problem and I lay and tossed in bed that night, unable to sleep, trying to find an answer. The following morning it was raining so combining was off, and

I took myself off up to the vets to have a good look at Kicker. Mary was busy around the yard.

"Good morning; it's OK; he had a good night," she called out. I was glad he had a good night; that was more than I had! "Tim's in the kitchen, go in." Tim and I kept bees and helped each other, often moving hives from place to place in the season. He was having a coffee and I joined him.

"I haven't seen the horse yet but after this, I will give it the once over for you. Where did you get it?" So I told him the story, that my girl's horse had to be put down and I had been given the pony to replace it, keeping the tale as short as possible. He made some toast and we talked of the bumper honey crop the year had produced. Then getting up, he got his van's keys and putting on his shoes, we left the warm pleasant smells of the kitchen for the loose boxes out in the yard. He got his scope from the van and hanging them around his neck, said,

"Now let's have a look shall we?" The pony watched us approach, with his head over the stable door, then, as Tim unbolted the door it went berserk. Mary rushed up,

"All right boys. Let me," and she took him by his halter, and smoothed his forehead with her hand. The animal instantly responded to a woman's touch.

"Got a good one here," Tim said. "No bloke is going to touch her on him; he's scared of men; something has upset him in his life. He's a bloody good Pinto by the look of it, worth a bob or two. Now let's have a listen," and Tim spent twenty minutes checking him out.

"First class," he said. "Where did you get him from?"

"I'm not saying," I said.

"Oh like that is it? Cost a lot did he, and don't want dad to know? OK. Bloody fine animal though! Go on forever they do; so intelligent too. The old cowboys out West used to kill for one of these," and I thought, 'I know someone closer to us than America who would kill if he knew who gave it to his precious girl!' That snag was to be overcome somehow.

We went back into the warm kitchen for another coffee and Tim's wife joined us. He told Mary the tale of me getting it for my girl

"She is a very lucky girl then. Who is she?" I had known Tim all my life; his family, were friends of ours. I thought it would be all right to enlighten them to the girl's family. As soon as I said who she was, he turned in his chair to look at me, and said,

"How long have you known her? Have you met the others? Talk about a bloody gypsy camp, full of old iron and rubbish; I don't know how the animals don't get more hurt on the place; they called me out one day a few years back. I had heard of them but didn't believe it, until that day I had to go to a cow of theirs." Tim lit his pipe and gave it a good drag to make the content flare. "The old man is mad, and the woman stood over me with a bat, like an executioner ready to strike if the cow died. It had a bit of wire in its throat, horrid nasty job it was, but thank God the cow lived! Otherwise I think I would still be up there now, pushing up daises!"

He struck another match, but the tobacco refused to fire up so he flung the pipe on the table, uttering "Bloody thing.

They have an older son, nasty bit of work, broken nose, a real fighter, proper gypsy type of family. That pony is right up their street if the girl is anything like the lot I saw. Two or three little boys they've got and a lovely little girl with long brown hair, about eight years old. Is she the one the pony's for?"

"No; there is a girl of seventeen with jet black hair."

"Didn't see her," said Tim fiddling with his pipe again,

"But I get the picture. If they say, keep away, you emigrate John. Those sorts of people have friends. I don't envy you giving her father that pony out there for their daughter. Good luck; hope to see you again! But don't involve the wife or me; we never did get paid for the cow job." He struck another match and paused and the flame died out. "Sod." he said, and tossed it in the empty coffee cup and lit another then with out waiting tried to light the pipe. "How do you intend to get the animal to the girl without them knowing? It stands out a mile!"

"That's the problem at the moment; I was thinking along the lines of an anonymous well-wisher."

"Good idea; that would be your safest bet."

"Yes I know, but I only found out the old pony had gone by accident. You see the whole family never leave the farm except the mother on market day and then never talk's to anyone, so how will the well-wisher know she needs a new pony?"

"I've no idea John; they could have seen it missing from the field."

"Yes, but no-one will speak to you if you asked the whereabouts of it so you wouldn't know. They never go to a pub or talk."

"Is there no-one who knows them who you could talk to?" The vision of Mrs. Wilton flashed to my mind.

"One," I said. "Is it all right to leave Kicker with you for a while?"

"As long as you like," said Mary.

"Thanks," I said and left.

It was still a wet old morning as I drove into the yard of Land Farm. Mike was in the guts of a huge combine in one of the sheds as I got out the car.

"In here," He called out. I climbed up on the machine alongside him.

"Trouble?" I said.

"Nothing a bloody good hammer won't put right!" he said, and gave one of the beater bars a clout. "Picked half a brick up yesterday; got in the drum, and made a hell of mess before it broke up. What are you doing out here? Mandy's not here and Sally's away for a week; gone down to Cornwall to her Aunt's."

"Mike; don't tell Alan anything about me please. If it gets back to Mandy's parents there could be trouble."

"I know," he said. "Don't worry about Alan; he's as safe as houses; he won't talk, mark my words. It's you we are worried about. That family! My God, they are strange. I went up there once, never again. All the kids in rags, everything dirty won't have a cup of tea up there. Come on; mum should have the coffee on by now and a wedge of cake," and he slammed the hatch back on the threshing drum and kicked the retaining bolts in place. The warmth of the kitchen hit me as we walked into the room. Mrs. Wilton had the two mugs out on the table ready.

"Saw you two coming John. To what do we owe the pleasure?"

"That's tricky," I said. "How well do you know Mandy's family?"

"Not very well at all now," she said, "but when the kids were small, Mandy's mum and I were real pals. They lived in our old orchard on our old farm up in Kent in a caravan like real gypsies. Sally and Mandy played together; you never saw one without the other. Then we came here." She poured two cups of coffee, and sat down to look at me. "It seems that there was some trouble after we left, Mandy's dad was mixed up in some crime or other never did find out what, then they turned up where they are now. The girls then met up again at school Sally could leave this term but has gone back till Easter trying to get a pass. She is not very academic, not like Mandy. She's very clever, studying law of all things." Mrs Wilton did not look happy telling me all this in front of her son and kept looking at him as if trying to get some clue as to if he knew anything. "When the other children were born, Mandy's mum stopped speaking to me for some reason but she still let the girls play together. Now she remembers the girls were friends and lets Mandy stay most weekends." Michael got up from his chair and went to the cake on the draining board and cut another wedge for himself.

"My husband has his own thoughts on the matter but we wont go into that. It saves her mother food and train fares staying here weekends other than that, I know nothing. You know Mandy has little in the way of clothes; the only new ones are yours. Mrs Wilton's face smiled, "I've seen them up in Sally's room. I sat and looked at them the other day. Reminded me of when I was courting your dad Michael. Mandy is so happy when she comes and you are going out. There's a little sister as well in the family."

"Mandy never told me that," I said lying

"Yes; about eight. Mandy does not speak of her." "I wonder if there is anything wrong with her? I don't ask; it is a very strange set up in her home."

"I know," I said, "but I have a problem. Mandy lost her pony last week and I have a new one for her, but don't know how to give it to her." Shirley got the coffee pot from the top of the Aga.

"Lost her pony?"

"Yes; her father shot it."

"Poor girl," Sally said. Mandy had told her it was lame; I never knew it was that bad. Poor girl; she loved that pony. That was the only freedom she had I think, and you have got a replacement?"

"Yes, but how do I give it to her?"

"That is a big one? It's Mandy's birthday next month. What's the date today? Twenty eighth August. Yes; on the eighteenth of September we could have a party; it could be a birthday present. Give it to her then."

"I can't," I said. "They will want to know how I know her."

"That's true. I tell you what; we could give it as a present from the Wilton's."

"Of course!"

"We will tell Mandy it is nothing to do with us. We can then give her some lovely clothes, that way the parents need not know."

"Where's the animal now then John?" asked Michael.

"At a mate's in a stable," I said.

"Well Sally is home this Friday; why don't you give it to Mandy this weekend?"

"Now there is a horse sale on this week in the market." Said Michael. "Dad could say it came from there; we have no grass to keep it on she can have it as an early present to get to know it.

"Michael that's a brilliant idea his mother said."

"I know a mate who has a cattle lorry and will drop it off for ten shillings. Mandy's dad can't say no. My mate can say he did not know the fellow who paid him he doesn't have to say who it was from or where he got it, just that a man paid him in the market to deliver it; like every other farmer who buys animal they all use hire lorries to take the animals home."

"Michael, that is a marvellous ploy."

"There John; your problem is solved."

Mrs. Wilton suddenly thought, "But how do we know the old pony is no longer with us? Sally's been away for two weeks, and has had no contact with Mandy."

"Sod!" said Mike. "That's put a spanner in the works. We will have to keep it stabled until Mandy comes this week and has the chance to tell Sally. Is that all right John?"

"Fine, I said. When does Mandy arrive here?"

"Friday night usually but as it's holiday, Saturday about ten am. Usually has to get the bus from Appledore."

"Mrs. Wilton?"

"Shirley please!"

"Maybe I could show the pony to Mandy on Saturday if the two girls are here?"

"Of course," said Shirley. "I won't tell Sally, and Michael don't you dare say anything either!"

"No mum. Of course not!"

I was so relieved the problem was solved. The now cold coffee flowed down my throat; a wonderful feeling came over me. I left and the rain had stopped. I made my way home after going back to the vets but they were out. I found dad with one of the men at home and asked for the weekend off again.

"It's a girl at last, eighteen and never looked at one before," said dad. "Now it's time off all the time! Alright. We will manage won't we George?" and the old man folding sacks with dad winked at me and gave a deep draw on his fag as if to say, 'I was once there like you my boy!' and a twinkle came into his eye.

"Soon be a wedding Ern!" He said to my father, and carried on folding up the dusty old sacks, ready for the combining that we hoped to start again tomorrow.

CHAPTER NINE

The following morning we attacked twelve acres of thick standing oats and it went well. By night we had three hundred and forty sacks laying out on the stubble ready to be loaded and hauled back to the barn. The modern loose bulk corn combine was still five years away from us; all our corn was harvested with a bagger combine and dropped from the machine, as we went in piles of eight bags, but we did have help in the evening. Four lads came and on an old TVO tractor and trailer soon had them loaded and home safely stacked on the driers and with the tops untied and rolled down warm air was forced up through them, so removing the water content to ten per cent to stop them overheating with combustion or going mouldy. That done it was eat, bath and bed until the same the next day when we went into the wheat.

The weekend was approaching and I phoned Sally at nine on Friday night. She was surprised to hear from me. She had had a lovely time with her niece and aunt. Now she was looking forward to tomorrow night when she said, "Was I going to surprise them again?" Mandy had phoned her an hour ago and she was going to ask me tomorrow to take her out. I left it at that and did not tell her I was coming in the morning. As a thought at the very last moment, Sally said, "You don't know the sad news do you?"

"What?" I said.

"Poor Mandy lost her pony the other day. She is heartbroken and does not know how she is going to see you any more in the evenings."

"Don't worry," I said. "I will sort it out."

"You can't. The poor thing is dead!" and Sally slammed the phone down thinking I did not care that the pony was no longer with Mandy.

The next morning at eight I was up the vets talking to Mary; she said she would be in all day and would love to see the girls. So I left for Land Farm. It was a glorious day; dad and the men would get on well harvesting to day; the corn and straw was dry. Soon I pulled into the yard and the girls ran out to see me. Mandy was all over me.

"Missed you Darling," she said and Sally gave me a knowing wink. She knew of the pony; someone had told her. I found out later that after last night's little episode on the phone she had thrown a tantrum about the fact that I seemed not to care that Mandy's pony was dead so her mother had told her of the surprise today.

"I wish we could go out for a drive," Sally said.

"Well, we could," I said, "if you want."

"Let's go now," said Sally in just as much of a hurry as I was to show Mandy Kicker.

"Ok," said Mandy. "Where to?"

"Let's go and turn right out of the drive and see where it goes," I said. "Come on," I noticed Shirley standing at the kitchen window with a broad smile on her face taking in the rapid exodus of the girls.

"Turn right," said Mandy, and swept her long hair over the back of her head into Sally's face who was none to pleased by it.

"You and your hair, have you never had it cut? It is full of split ends."

"Leave my hair alone, Ox loves it."

"You will get lost in it one day," Sally said and pushed her head between us in the front as if to see clearer. Rye came up soon and Mandy wanted to know where we were going as we were now getting into her home territory and she did not wish to be seen.

We drove up Rye Hill, turned left, then took a private lane and she started to relax.

"How far does this go?" the girls asked."

"Not far, only I have to see a fellow, but it won't take a jiff. Mary heard us stop and came out of the house.

"Hello you girls. Didn't expect you John until this afternoon. Never mind; he's in number Four John."

"What is?" said Mandy to Sally," who was already getting out the car.

"Go and see Mandy," I said. "All yours." She looked at me.

"Mine?" but did not have time to say anything else.

"Come on," said Sally. "He's yours, for keeps!" They left the car doors open for me to shut and were gone. Forty feet away a black and white head showed over the stable door that now had chalked on it, **'Kicker. With love from John.'** Good old Mary! And I thanked her.

"Not my doing," she said. "That was Tim's idea."

Mandy turned to look at me.

"Is he really mine?"

"Yes, I heard about David."

"Can I go inside with him?"

"You do what you want", said Mary; he loves a fuss being made of him." The bolts were slammed back and the pony pushed his way out, unwilling to wait for the girls to enter. Mandy stood and looked at him, then burst into tears. The pony responded by taking a mouthful of her black hair in his mouth and waved his head up and down as if pulling hay from a hay-net.

"Don't do that," she snapped at him and he let go, her tears now forgotten.

"Get up on him," Sally said. "Let's see you on his back." Mandy left the ground, gripping his mane with her left hand. He did not bat an eyelid. She looked a picture, her hair reaching his back.

"Take him for a trot," said Mary, who had been watching the three get to know each other. Mary opened the gate from the yard into a fifteen-acre field that sloped down to the old heronry in the gill at the bottom.

"Gee up," spoke Mandy, and flicked his side with her new brown shoes, her skirt new the other week, now covered in horse hairs! He picked his hooves up and they trotted to the gate; then Mandy put him through his paces. The earth flew from his hooves. They were gone!

"I hope she knows how to stop him," Sally said, running up to Mary and I standing watching the two fly across the field.

"Oh she knows," said Mary. "They are made for each other and she knows how to ride." They vanished down the bank over the far side, the pony and a trail of black hair that hid the rider. We heard them coming back in front of the house before we saw them. Mandy was talking to him and he was panting and snorting in time to his feet. Mary said, he was a musical pony and did that like a lot of breeds to show you how easy it was. She said, he could go on all day at the rate they were moving and that is why the cowboys loved steeds like that, chasing cattle all day and being ready the next to go again.

As they had come up the bank in front of the house, Tim saw them from the drawing room window and left his coffee to join us.

"I'd like to have a look at him after this," he said, "but I'm sure he is fine, and I'll take a look at that girl if you like John!"

"Tim you behave yourself! I'm telling you, keep your sordid remarks to yourself," said Mary. " Take no notice of him."

"I don't," I said, and Sally blushed as Tim was giving her the once over with his eyes.

Mandy pulled Kicker round and trotted to the gate where we four stood.

"I love him," she said. "Is he really mine?"

"Yes darling; all yours."

"I can't accept him," she said. "You give me too much."

Mary chipped in "Don't complain young lady. Get all you can.

He can afford it; loaded he is!" And I thought to myself 'I wonder where they get their ideas from?'

There's a saddle in the tack room Tim said "lets see if it fits him come on I would like to sound him out after a gallop like that, just to be on the safe side," Mandy slid off his back and tried to climb all over me in front of everyone.

"I love you," kissing me all the time. I was embarrassed and showed it.

"Stop it!" I said. "You like it!" Mandy said, and I went redder.

Tim took the pony to a rail and tied him up with the halter that Mandy had used to ride him with. I was proud of her. A few minutes later Tim bent up straight from sounding the pony with his stethoscope.

"Marvellous, sound as a bell, a good animal that. Now let's look at this saddle." He moved over to the door of the tack room and appeared with a new cowboy saddle with a big pommel, all made in white leather with a fantastic pattern of flowers engraved all over it. He slung it on the animal's back and the pony only moved one back leg forward one inch or two. It fitted like a glove.

"Go on girl; try that." He said bending up straight from buckling the girth straps up Mandy's amazed expression turned to a smile and she looked at me.

"Another present?"

"No, nothing to do with me," I said. She took a firm grip with her left hand on the pommel and threw her right leg over the saddle, revealing a pair of white knickers that I knew to be new. Then bending forward to grab the single rope halter dangling from Kickers chin she vanished under a mass of black hair, to appear smiling and fumbling for the stirrups. Mary ran over and shortened them on the straps.

"There we are," she said. "Go!" And boy did they go! The two came through the gate at a canter and galloped off across the field with Mandy's left arm flinging in the air like a cowboy in a rodeo.

"Showing off now," said Sally, looking a little sad. She would love to have a gift as well, I thought.

"Well they are fine John," Tim said. "Now have you solved the problem of getting her old woman to let her keep it?"

"We think so," said Sally in a fluster of words and I let her have a say in this morning's events. "It's going to be her eighteenth birthday in a few days and dad is going to pretend it's from us."

"That's a wonderful idea," said Mary, "and Tim has given her the saddle as a birthday present as he likes the girl. Right Tim?" He looked hurt.

"Of course I have; she can keep it. Ann hasn't got a pony yet for it to fit. Silly of me to buy it before the horse, only I liked the look of it, so did my daughter, but she will not mind. I suppose I will have to buy her a new one again now."

"Good," said Mary." Come on, coffee. Let's leave the young blood to get acquainted." We entered the house to watch from the dining room window. The coffee arrived; Tim slid the huge patio doors aside and we sat outside watching the two having fun. Mandy rode up to the garden fence, then with her arm up, swung him round in a turn no longer than his body, then she brought him to a standstill and he went down on his knees and prayed.

"That pony has been circus trained!" Tim exclaimed. "Where did you find it?" So I told the three of them the facts making them promise not to tell Mandy, without disclosing that Mandy had said they were her family. Tim lit his little pipe up full of Erinmore Tobacco and made clouds of smoke.

"From some gypsies you say. I bet it's stolen."

"Don't say that," his wife said. "There's no registration mark on it and its ears are clean, no sign of a tattoo."

"At the moment," said Tim. "Yes maybe, but we will alter that when she gets back. What's the girl's name John?"

"Mandy", I said, "Why?"

"That's all right then," he said. "Easy; we will freeze brand it when Mandy gets back from her circus act, with the letters MA O2, as it's her second pony. Then the real owner won't have a claim on it." He took the pipe from his mouth gave the bowl a quizzing look and clamped it back between his teeth and sucked hard, nothing happened so he put it down on the table. "A horse like that is very expensive and most people would insist on a mark. I can't really believe it's not stolen, knowing who it's from but the person who broke it in knew what he was doing. Look at it go!" The pair were out in the field for over half an hour; then we went out to meet them as they ventured to the stable.

"OK Mandy. Does the saddle feel all right?"

"It's lovely. I have never ridden a horse with a saddle. I learned to ride on a cow when I was little and dad never bought me a saddle. He will be so jealous. It's a lovely colour."

"It suits you Mandy," said Mary. "Now we must brand Kicker so no one can steal him. Tim thought the letters MA and the numbers O2 because it is your second pony."

"Don't hurt him will you?"

"No, it's only very cold for a few seconds. Look," and he held an iron brand that had stood in a canister of steaming liquid nitrogen that he had handy from a job yesterday marking a herd of cows. The pony hardly flinched as the brand left its mark on his right flank.

"There, all yours," Tim said. Sally was nearly in tears, the branding of the pony left her in no doubt it was Mandy's. I had to get her something also for sure, but what? I thought I had better talk to Mandy when we were on our own; as I did not want to make her jealous if I gave Sally a gift. We went indoors as Mandy wanted the toilet and Sally accompanied her like girls do; it seems to be a two women job! We all got talking when the girls came back. What was Mandy's dad going to say if Mr. Wilton gave her an expensive pony? And Mandy said, "He would be over the moon, especially if she was nice to him in their special way." Tim and I looked at each other. I thought she must mean a lot of sewing and darning his old socks. The coming evening sprang up in conversation and I said what would the girls like to do.

"Dancing," Mandy said, and Sally said, "John cannot afford to buy more clothes after the pony so don't expect him to."

"Yes I can," I said. What do you want?" Sally looked even more despondent. I had to get her something soon.

"OK," I said, "Where are we going dancing then?" Mary was taking a lot of interest in the conversation and said to Tim

"When did we last go dancing? Why don't we go tonight and treat John and the girls? You are a member of the King's Club in Eastbourne. Can you girls stay?"

"I don't know," said Sally.

"We'll ring your mum and ask; what's their number? I'm sure they will let you join us. Tim is your dad's vet." Sally rang her mum and got her dad; he was in the house waiting to see Mandy and ask if she liked the pony. He said if they were with the vet and his wife, he saw no problems. Then Mary had a word and it was arranged that as they were already at Rye, they were half way there; she would feed them and tonight they could sleep at the house. John would come and collect them tomorrow and take them back to Land Farm. He acknowledged the arrangements and Mary said it was a pleasure to have them. She hung up and turned her face smiling to say they could stay the night so could stay out late. Tim would drive the Rover car, there was plenty of room for five of us, but first new clothes; and on that remark Tim took his wallet out.

"How much?" he said. "Twenty pounds do?" I had a keystone now to work from. That meant forty pounds from me if I was to clothe both girls tonight. I got my wallet out and put my forty pounds on the table; that only left me five pounds, I a farmer was never going to be able to keep up with him a vet. Poor old Tim had to go upstairs to get more money as his wallet only had ten pounds in it. He arrived downstairs to hand over the money and kiss Mary goodbye and the two girls left with his wife to spend our money. Mandy felt safe in Rye with Mary. So long as no boys were present.

Tim and I decided to take some of his dogs for a walk. The girls appeared at three, well satisfied with the trip. Mary had a new outfit and Sally had a new blouse and that solved the problem of a gift for Sally now she did not feel so left out. Mandy had a new skirt as the one she wore was covered in pony hair, and a top that hung from the shoulders on little thin straps. "She had been bullied," she said, "by the other two, to have her hair trimmed in a real shop in a big chair, to have it washed by a woman and all the split ends removed." Now her hair was only forty-two inches long and the girl in the shop told her that if ever she wanted it off, they would buy it. She also had a new item that she had never possessed before in her life; 'a purse', and she was proud of it, especially as it held the girls change that they said was hers. The nine pounds it held was more money than she'd ever had and she was not going to spend it.

So everyone was set and with three hours to kill, Mandy and I decided that as the sun shone from a clear sky and it was warm, we would like to go for a walk on our own. Sally said, "Go on; enjoy yourselves."

She was happy with Mary. Mandy took my arm and we set off along the hedge of the fifteen acres that she knew well from her trips around on Kicker. Mandy cuddled in to me as we strolled slowly along the bottom past the heronry and out on to the bank where half way up stood a large silver birch whose leaves were now changing colour with the approach of autumn. We lay down and I took my jacket off for her to put under her newly washed hair that shone like liquid tar. The sun shone on her amber dark skin tanned by the wind. Her dark eyes explored everything. She marvelled at the shadows of the clouds, which stole the sunlight from the soil as they passed over our heads, sweeping across the rising ground to the north turning the swaying acres of distant corn still awaiting the reaper a shade more golden. Then they jumped from the hilltop to pass out of sight into the valley on the other side, only to be chased by more of the same.

It was a glorious day and I was alone with the girl I loved. She brushed her skirt, that was covered in pony's hair, and then gently pulled it up her thighs and slipped her knickers off. I watched fascinated

"John, be careful with me." I looked at her exquisite body, not ready to see the girl like this, so unashamed in daylight. I lay and kissed her on the mouth. She was rigid, in a sort of trance.

"Mandy. What is the matter with you?"

"Nothing," she said. "I love you; go on, do it."

"What?" I said in a low voice.

"Have me like you want."

"I don't 'want', as you put it."

"All men do," she said. "Mum says so."

"Bugger your mum; not all men are after the same thing like that," I said. "Pull your skirt down," and I pulled it down to cover her bottom.

"Don't you know how to?" she said with a tear in her eye, "I will have to show you," and she placed her hand in my trousers.

"That's OK," she said. This was too much; I rolled over on to her so she could feel through our clothes how much I did want her, "Mandy, Darling that's not love. That is sex, not making love; it's not a thing you have to do; you can love for all sorts of reasons. I love you but again like the first night, you are throwing yourself at me." And I felt her whole body go soft as she once again relaxed.

"My mum and dad say that it is all girls are any good at and that's all men want."

"Now listen sweetheart! I am sorry but I think they are wrong, it should come when we are both ready and I will prove it to you one day but not now. I bet you are good but I don't think now is the time to find out."

"But I am good; I know how to make it good," and she stopped and started to cry, real floods of tears that meant something that was in the past, nothing to do with now. I hugged and caressed her. Her hands showed mine the way to go; she got a lot of pleasure just from that and we both had fun.

The old sun was dipping down to the hilltops; a nip was in the air as I pulled her up to her feet and she thanked me for being so soft with her. It had been good, so good, no sex or pain. She loved me and we slowly walked, as lovers do, back to the house and I thought, 'No pain;' what did she expect and what idea had she got from her mother and father that she had to throw her body at men? She surely was still a virgin at seventeen. If she thought it was painful, having had no contact with boys other than me, what had she been told? She had been brought up to believe that it was a Romany's role alone to slave for a man, and be on call for his needs whenever he thought fit, and she with no right to refuse him. That was the picture I was getting. If so, it was up to me to show her she was wrong and educate her in the times of the nineteen sixties. Her perception was thousands of years out of date; that went out with the cavemen and their clubs.

CHAPTER TEN

The others were getting dinner ready when we entered after saying goodnight to Kicker and making sure he had hay and water for the night.

"Here come the lovebirds," Sally said, as we entered the room. Mandy's hair was full of yellow golden leaves.

"Nice walk was it?"

"Yes, lovely," I said. "Right round the bank," I lied.

"Good sunset" said Mary.

Tim carved the lump of beef up into thick slices. Mary's food was good and we all ate a good fill. The girls had wine as well and Mandy was impressed even more when Mary bought out a large apple pie, all home made, not like the shop bought ones today. This one had an old eggcup to hold the middle up and let the steam out. Tim and I washed up as the girls went upstairs to get ready to go out. I borrowed Tim's razor and aftershave, had a wash and was already to go and dance the night away. The old moon had a few days still to go until he vanished and the stars outshone him in the galaxies above as we got in the car. Mandy had her arm around me and lay on my shoulder in the back seat, all the way to the club in Eastbourne, the home of a large holiday camp. All five of us danced our legs off that night all the ladies looked a million dollars, so young and agile. The Rock 'n' Roll and Jive was the dance of the fifties into the early sixties parts of our legs and arms flew all ways, so did we boys and girls, enjoying the times.

Around eleven that night a lad of eighteen to nineteen, took a fancy to Mandy and put his hand up her short skirt to pinch her bottom. The response he got from Mandy was instant and long lasting. She swung around to face him and gave his face one almighty slap that made him stagger back a pace.

"Steady on old girl!" he said.

"Touch me once more," she screeched, "and you are dead!" Her face drew tight and her eyes, those pools of dark brown, were now only slits of sparkling coal. She grabbed his left hand by the wrist, and wrenched it palm uppermost to her face and spat into it. "Do that again and I promise you your life will be hell. A curse on you!" and swore at him in a foreign tongue that I did not understand. "Only one man can have me and it's never going to be you. Now a curse on you and your family!" She threw his hand back at him, turned to smile at me and placed her arms around my neck.

"I love you," she said. "I am only for you to use." And we danced on. The boy was talking to his mates and they were glancing our way. I was staggered at what I had just witnessed. Mandy had put a curse on the lad and told me that I was the only one that could **use** her. For what purpose I had no idea? I knew the gypsies made all their women do all the work, but I had no intention of letting my girl work. It bothered me to think that my Mandy had placed a wicked curse on him. The face on this joyful girl at the time was not the happy one I knew. It had looked evil and the boy had sensed it as well. He and his mates kept looking at his hand and he never stopped trying to wipe the dreaded spit from his hand up the side of his trouser leg, as if Mandy's mouth had contained acid. The gypsy part of Mandy was alive and well but I did not wish her to use her spells on anyone.

We five left the place of pleasure at midnight and I drove us home in Tim's car. Sally and Mandy chatted in the back of the pony and what they could do tomorrow. Mary, Tim and I talked of the night, the scene they had witnessed of the boy and Mandy at the club. Also how the corn was coming off, and had we much more to cut? The road soon led to Rye and home. Mandy and I spent ten minutes out in the stable checking the pony and kissing, then it was to bed for her, and home for me. The last words from my darling were to thank me from the bottom of her heart that I had not taken her.

No moon shone from the sky now as I lay in my bed at home and dreamed of to day. The sound of mum calling me awoke me.

"You up there, John? What happened to you last night?"

"Coming" I answered. It was nine o'clock and I had overslept. Mother was doing the washing and had decided to wash the trousers that I had worn last night. On checking the pockets for coins she had found Mandy's knickers which she had taken off in the afternoon on our walk, when we had laid on that bank of grass and been mesmerised by all the clouds shadows flying across the fields. The reason for Mandy's sharp reaction to the boy's hand up her skirt in the club last night took on a new meaning, as it was such an anti-social response from her. I had forgotten the item mother now held. Mandy had danced the night away unclad in the nether regions. That girl will get talked about in all the places those boys go I thought. Mother only said, "I will wash them, then you can return them tonight." So she knew to whom they belonged.

Sally had gone riding with Mandy on one of Tim's daughter's ponies with Mary and would not be back for an hour or two so Tim and I sat down, read the paper, and chatted over a cup of coffee.

"She's a smashing girl your Mandy. Never knew she existed," he said. "How did you find her?"

"Up our farm," I said. "Just rode up one day and said hello."

"I'll have to get a farm if they grow like that," he laughed. "She tells us that she is studying to become a lawyer. She has high hopes for herself, saying it's for her father to give him what ought to be rightfully his one day."

"Oh yes," I said. "He was cut out of his father's will and disowned by the family when he ran away to marry Mandy's mother."

"Can't blame a bloke for that if her mum was like Mandy. You could go to the other end of the earth for the likes of her. Such a body! Her shape is fantastic and her hair! How long is it? Here they come now; look."

We both stared out of the window as the three came charging across the field, dirt flying and my Mandy out in front, the pony's head down, pulling his flexing body along behind him, her hair all a cloud behind her head, trying to keep up. A tear welled in my eye; to think that in an hour I would have to take her back to Land Farm, then she would have to return to the drudgery of her home. We went out to meet them as they entered the yard. Mandy slid from the saddle and kissed me.

"He is so good; faster than all the rest and you should see him jump! He loves it!"

I placed my hand on her bum and was glad to feel that this morning she was properly clad and out of view from the posse I gave her leg a little tweak.

"You forgot to wear any last night," I said and she smiled.

"I know; when we got undressed last night I took my skirt off and Sally gasped. She wondered how you got them off without her knowing and what else did we do? Sally said you were a naughty boy!" We all chatted and they rubbed the ponies down with handfuls of straw, then let them out in a paddock and went into dinner.

That afternoon I returned the girls to Land Farm and had tea with Shirley who wanted to know how it went, she was glad with the response she received from us. I said goodbye outside with Mandy and left her in tears once again, our next meeting to be in two weeks time at her party.

I phoned Sally a few times through the week, to get news of my girl but Mandy was frightened to use the phone too much as her parents were suspicious of her, as her and Sally had not talked on the phone so much before. The days were dry and sunny; the combining was going well and we were getting on. I was on a combine; we had two this year (mine was an eight foot, six inch cut Massie Harris) when Mandy appeared in the corner of the field. I stood on the brakes and Derek, who was bagging the corn, went flying into the safety rail.

"Watch out!" He said as corn slopped out of the bag spout. "Who's that?" following my stare to the girl in a straw hat chewing a bit of rye grass.

"She, Derek," I said, "is to be my wife I hope. Now get lost and get more strings from the shed to tie the sacks with," and I turned the engine off. He got the hint and vanished, taking a short cut through the corn. She threw her blouse off into the air as she ran to me and we tossed ourselves into the last row of straw and vanished beneath.

"What did you do that for you imp?" I said when I got my mouth free from hers.

"So you knew who I was," she said. "I'm yours."

"Steady on; I have told you before, not now."

"I must please you," she said. "I have to, don't I?"

"Not like that you don't, why are you in such a hurry? Derek could have seen." She pulled her hair over her shoulders to cover up her exposed breasts. Derek had not got the message right. When I had said 'get lost,' I had literally meant it but unfortunately he reappeared ten minutes later.

"Got two hundred," he called out climbing up on the machine. "Where are you?" We lay still, buried under the straw.

"Now what's the matter?" she said.

"Your blouse is ten yards away where you threw it. You are only wearing that short pair of pants."

"They are shorts," she whispered.

"Maybe, but three sizes too small!"

"I love them; they make me feel free." My mate called "John" again and from where we were twenty yards away, could see him looking the other way. "Now!" I said, and we stood up. Mandy slung her hair behind her and slipped away across the stubble, the noise of the straw rustling under her fleeing feet making the boy with the strings look round.

"Where have you been?" he said. "I've been calling you for twenty minutes."

"Lying bugger," I said as I watched Mandy retrieve her white blouse and disappear into the hedge.

"She's naked!" he said. "No she's not," I said and climbed the ladder to the seat. I pressed the starter and the red beast burst into life.

"Hold tight!" I said and we cut on. Mandy stood the other side of the hedge and threw me a kiss as we turned to take another went of the still standing wheat. I did not see Mandy for the rest of the week but her father came one afternoon as we were finishing a four-acre block of wheat. My heart skipped a beat. What was his presence doing here? I was worried, but he soon put me at ease when he asked about the straw.

"How much do you want?"

"Not much, haven't got a lot of money."

"That's all right," I said, sensing a chance to see Mandy and make her dad a friend.

"Have what you want, we only burn it you know. I will bale it for you; only too pleased to get rid of it." His old jaw moved; he knew a good deal when he saw it.

"A thousand, two thousand bales; makes no difference to me," I said, "but you will have to cart it."

"No problem," he said, rubbing his hands on his trouser legs with glee. "I can make a stack in the yard, be good for the old cows this winter; make some good muck. Better than burning it."

"I will bale it up for you tomorrow if you like."

"Yer, I'll get my workers rounded up," and I wondered whom he had in mind, as he employed no one to my knowledge. The answer came next morning at Eleven o'clock. I had been baling for an hour, when I noticed an old tractor coming along the lane with a large four-wheel trailer that I recognized as Mr. Brignal's. Mandy's dad had borrowed it and aboard the trailer with four pitchforks rode his workforce, his wife, eldest son and Mandy holding two little boys by their hands as they sat with their legs dangling over the back. My Mandy was going to be working in the same field as me and I owned the field! I felt proud. They came in the gate and stopped at the first bale; then the tribe of workers went mad. Free straw! Talk about free for all! The trailer started to fill, Mandy gave me a sly glance and a nod to say hello, but no other way was she going to give the gang a clue. I stopped alongside the half filled trailer as I made for the gateway to bale the next field, Mandy's mother rushed me as I alighted from my mount.

"Is it OK to have this?"

"Yes, take the lot."

"Good," she said, and turned away with the advice that I did not disturb the workers. I got the message. 'Go away! We don't talk to strangers!' I got back on the tractor and left to bale the next lot. I saw the tractor leave the field as I was down the bottom of the other field. The women and boys stayed behind to lump the remaining bales into groups to load. The tractor returned soon with another empty trailer. I got off the tractor and unwound the tension springs on the bale chamber so as to make the bales less dense and lighter, I was not having my girl hump dirty great heavy bales of straw around all day! Another four-wheel trailer was soon filled. I stopped at five pm; four trailers had been loaded and I thought Mandy must be tired and would sleep well tonight.

Next day as I arrived back at the farm at ten the field laid bare, they had taken sixteen hundred bales in twenty-four hours! What a family! I hooked the bailer up to bale some lovely barley straw. I thought the cows would not go hungry this winter if they had a load of this. The tractor and the four-wheel trailer appeared empty with the workforce and got set in. Poor Mandy's hair was covered in barley awns by dinnertime, by the way she moved; I could see it was giving her a problem. Soon it would become a solid mat. I felt like moving into more amiable winter wheat so left the rest of the barley to burn later on. The cows could starve for all I cared; Mandy was my number one. The family relieved our farm of nine thousand bales of straw and their house was dwarfed by the huge straw stack that year that had risen alongside the road hedge.

The party weekend was coming up; school had started that week and Mandy had been absent from straw carting. The combining was over for another year and apple picking was now under way. I took myself off on Saturday at four, as the sun was now getting low in the sky. Winter was on its way and the day had seen the first real rain in five weeks. The sky was thick with cloud and it was going to get dark early tonight. I drove to Land Farm to meet my Mandy. Her eighteenth birthday was last week, but the Wilton's had decided that they had to make sure their harvest was over, before having a party so we were four days late celebrating the event. As the pony was not really from me, I could not let Mandy know that, so had got her a gold chain with her name on it in large gold letters, all set with little diamonds that sparkled. It had cost a lot of money, as it had to be made for me I had ordered it long before the pony had shown up. Now if I told her where the pony came from she would have kittens to know that the caravan folk knew of her whereabouts. The chain had come in a large black box lined in red velvet.

No one ran out as usual to meet me, which I found strange, but the reason was apparent as I entered the back door to poor old Mr. Wilton. I felt sorry for him, the only man in the house at the time and twelve girls running around. Shirley was in her element with so much female company and all the presents the girls had brought. Mandy spotted me and cried,

"There's Ox!" and she forced her way through the crowd of women. I held my arms out to receive her and we kissed our greeting. There stood my Mandy in new clothes that the Wilton's had given her. She turned around to show me a knee length pleated skirt and white blouse.

"Do you like them?" and I noticed that she had managed to get all the barley awns from her hair. "Nearly perfect," I said.

"What do you mean, nearly?" Her dark eyes piercing and all

seeing looking into my face with evil intent and disappointment. "Don't you like it?"

"Well there's only one thing missing."

"I'm wearing some!"

"No, not them, this," and as the crowd of girls were still trying to work out what was missing, I gave her my present wrapped in pink paper. Mandy tore the paper off to reveal the box and opened it. Mrs. Wilton shouted for her husband to come.

"Look at what he has gone and bought her!" The whole room gave a gasp of amazement at the beauty of the jewels that Mandy held up. Tears ran down her cheeks and she drew the back of her hand across her face to remove the moist salty droplets. For the first time Mandy was speechless she swallowed a lump in her throat then looking up from the chain in her fingers looked at me.

"I love you. Please put them on for me," and amid the clapping of hands from the well-wishers who all sang 'Happy Birthday to you'. I fumbled my way around her neck under the piles of hair to secure the chain. Her long neck led your eyes to the film star like looks. Mrs. Wilton gave her husband a hug of satisfaction. All was well for Mandy.

Food and drink abounded at the party and with me the only boy, my time was spent talking and explaining my work and how I had found Mandy. Boys were not allowed at the party, as a lot of the girls were friends of Mandy from her school and being an all girls boarding school, they were not allowed to talk or have contact socially with boys. That had been part of the agreement the school had insisted on. Sally's Martin came at seven pm and just after that a minibus collected the group of girls so the remaining six of us decided that the pub was the place to be now Mandy was eighteen, it was now legal for her to drink. Mr. and Mrs. Wilton took three girls and I took Mandy and Sally. The Wiltons decided a pub in Folkestone was safe enough from the eyes of Mandy's parents just for once.

The bar was well patronised but not crowded until Mandy walked in; then word went out, 'You should see the girl in the public bar', and all the other bars crowded in. She was the attraction of all the attention tonight. Her name stood out in sparkling relief. Who could not notice Mandy? And it was her birthday so the drinks flowed.

Mr. and Mrs. Wilton left at ten with two of the girls, leaving their daughter with Martin and Mandy and me. Mandy was the star of the night and whereas at other times her hair had been the talking point, tonight it was the jewels around her neck. Around eleven, someone foolishly bought us a large bottle of champagne, with the cork out, in a bucket of ice. The purchaser gave it to Mandy, wishing her a 'Happy Birthday' and left. Obviously by the dress of him, the man was one of the people from the private bar who had come through to have a gawp at the princess. So many people had seen her tonight and with the hair and her name up in sparkling stones around her neck, word was likely to get back to our part of the woods. I prayed it would not. Mandy now decided she rather liked the champagne and was drinking it like water,

"Time to go", I said to Martin. So we left with Mandy clutching the half empty bottle close to her body.

On entering the yard, we coasted up behind the barn with the lights out and parked up. Sally and Martin were entangled on the back seat, so Mandy and I sought out our usual straw stack. We came close that night to making real love but the drink was in the way. No way was I going to take my girl into wonderland in the state she was in, then making sure she still had her necklace on we got Sally, and I took them to the back door. 'Now don't lose that,' I said. Sally said she would look after it until she could take it to her own safe place, whenever that would be. I returned to the car and Martin, now no better off for wear, as he had finished the large bottle that Mandy had discarded earlier.

CHAPTER ELEVEN

The pony was delivered on Monday morning as arranged, and Mr. Wilton had a phone call from Mandy's mother to thank them.

"It was a good healthy animal and they would keep it; she presumed the saddle was from Sally as it was rather gaudy, being all white. "Thank you," and that was the lot. No mention of the party Sally told me, when she rang that night to say all had gone well as planned. Mandy had done well at school and decided to stay on until Christmas when a seat came up at Oxford University for her. The date given was the second of January 1961. She was thrilled for Mandy but sad for me as it meant a separation for us. She said she could see a change in Mandy's outlook on life, she had a feeling that Mandy was not happy with everything. It was just a feeling; things were not as they should be. She could not put her finger on it, had I seen the change? There was something awfully wrong.

"Mandy so much wanted to go away from home but did not want to leave me" I said "she was growing up, that was all," and we left it at that and hung up.

I pondered the meaning of a change and thought I could see it had started from the day we went to Canterbury Cathedral. I took my thoughts a step further. 'The gypsies'. Yes, she had said "My family". Was she really a full-blooded one? Did her parents steal her when young? That made sense as her brothers had much lighter skin and hair. The little sister I had never seen so did not know anything of. I wondered was it the gypsies that were upsetting Mandy? Sally was concerned over something. I said my prayers for Mandy and went to sleep.

The week was going well. I saw the pony up in the field by the road every day I went to our outlying farm; the apple picking was nearly finished for another year. The next job was the ploughing to tackle. That evening the phone rang for me as I was leaving for the pub.

"It's Sally. How are you? I have a message for you. Please be at the Lime tree tomorrow, NOON."

"Yes of course."

"I'm sorry John but that is all she said. Mandy is very moody at present. Something is wrong you know; it's to do with her at home I'm sure. Must go now; love you," and she rang off.

The old lime tree at mid-day, in the day light it had to be serious. Mandy wanted to meet me but what was it that she was so moody about? The girl had won a scholarship to university and was so young; she should be so happy. I shut the front door of the house, and drove the old van to the pub. All the gang were there and I joined them with my pint of coke. The subject of the wayward pony came up and they all had a laugh.

"Couldn't find it John, could you and it was right under your nose, only next door having a drink. Took a woman to find it for you and how is it on the girl front? Don't see you out much with women. You've got to have a girl you know or are you a poofter?"

"Don't be silly he has a girl" Alan said and then thought better of it and gave me a knowing look of apology.

"Sorry mate; forgot. How are you? How's that pony? Found it a home yet?"

"All taken care of," I said.

"Bloody hell! How do you do it? One day, you wait and see; the whole bloody thing will blow up in your face, you mark my words. It will be in all the papers, the lot. How the Gypsies stole the baby, now the rich lad has stolen the poor girl from them all the lies and deceit. Keep away John now."

"I am doing nothing lawfully wrong Alan, "The girl is

eighteen; there really is nothing they can do, and she's going to university next year, so we will not see each other very often. She will meet someone else I know that; she is too pretty for me; you should see her dressed up."

"You don't dress them John; the idea is to get their clothes off. There is no hope for you is there? You have it all arse about cock. What university is she going to then?"

"Oxford."

"Bloody hell! What is she going to do?"

"Law of all things."

"Christ! That's posh. She that bright then?" I flew in her defence.

"Yes she is. She's not just a pretty face; she wants to give her father his just desserts for being robbed by his father, so is going to concentrate on the legal side to try and overturn the disowned bit I think." Alan looked at his empty glass and said.

"I don't want to know. Do my head in all that law stuff. Come on get the beer in and let's play darts." We played darts until we were kicked out at closing time.

Next day I made myself scarce up the outlying farm and wandered up to the old lime tree now standing stark against the sky, high up on the bank, all the leaves now gone with the chilly winds of the approaching winter. The odd pigeon left its branch with a sudden clap of wings, and the old blackbird gave his warning call, as I walked up the headland of the field now lying in bare plough awaiting the frost to turn it into a seedbed. The leaves of the hedgerow bushes rustled under my feet.

The huge Lime tree did not look as inviting now for a romantic romp as it did in high summer. The adjoining cherry orchard was cold looking. All the trees stood in long lines amid rows of tired looking grass, their smooth bark trying to give off a shine in the low sun and this was the top of the day; it would get no better than this weather wise. November was but three weeks old, but my mood changed as I thought of Mandy soon to join me. I walked around under the tree; the ground was covered in seeds of the fruit and wet leaves fallen from its canopy. No way were we going to lay here and hug or kiss. A new winter venue was called for, but I had no time to think of that as I heard the sound of a girl's voice singing 'I'm the last of the Irish Rovers, and the Old wooden cross'.

Mandy came slowly riding along the hedge of the orchard. Kicker carrying my love to me. He flicked his ears on seeing me but Mandy made no effort to spur him on; she was in no hurry to see me for some reason. I stood waiting out on the verge of the plough as if I was a cowboy in the street waiting for the first man to draw. Something was wrong. She drew up and gave me a smile.

"Ox; I knew you would come. You never let me down. Now help me off." I put my hands up to get her down; she slid from the saddle to the ground and gave me a kiss. I held the pony by its bridle and went to tie him up. He stepped back and lifted his front leg in the air, pulling the bridle from my grasp and galloped off. "Kicker!" Mandy called out and he turned and wandered back.

"He won't let a man near him but you don't have to tether him."

"Here boy," she took his reins and tossed them over his neck. "He is OK on his own, so good. Where did you get him darling?"

"Never mind him, it's you I'm worried about. What's the matter with you? I noticed a difference in you coming along then," nodding my head in the direction she had just come. "You were slow; that's not like you."

"It's nothing, just a little tummy ache; don't feel myself today so have taken today of school. Really there's nothing wrong; going to have a cold maybe." I said nothing of my conversation the other night with Sally on the phone,

"Come on Ox. Where did that pony come from? He knows so many tricks. Mum and Dad have had to go out so I have had the day off school to look after the house."

"Come Mandy; we must talk," and we found an old ash stub in the wood to sit on.

"I must tell you the truth. I gave you only that necklace with your name for your birthday. The pony was from the gypsies," Mandy jumped up.

"From who?" she shouted. "The gypsies! You bought him from the gypsies!"

"Sit down Mandy. No; I never said that I paid for him; they gave him to you."

"Why? I don't know any gypsies." "You do, we met them the day we went to Canterbury didn't we?"

"Them!" she said. "They were my mother's relations, one was my mothers sister."

"Your aunt and mum's relations! You never said Mandy. Why didn't you tell me?"

She looked frightened and startled, "I can't tell you everything," she said in a sad voice, "how did they find me?"

"They never found you," I said, "only Alan and I found them a week later."

"Alan? Who's Alan?"

"A mate of mine you know his brother."

"What's his surname?

"Aldridge, the ones from Peasmarsh, the builders. You know them?

"I don't know Alan, I only know Rodney he comes on the train to Ashford. Mum was a friend of his mother when we were small but now they don't talk. Mum won't speak to anyone. But how did the gypsies know of me and you?"

"They don't; only when Alan and I saw them they recognised me, followed us back, and found him later in the pub with me. Mandy looked frightened, but I told them nothing, only that I knew you had lost David, so the next evening they brought him," pointing to kicker," to the pub that's all they know, then I had to get him to you. I should have told you sooner, only I didn't know how to." She got up, went over to the pony and spoke to him in his ear. She was talking to him in her foreign language that she spoke so well, then after telling him "go," turned round to face me, her face a mass of tears.

"Darling, he is so special but you are more so to me," and threw her arms around me and gave me the hardest kiss anyone can ever experience. She then turned to Kicker and said something in the foreign language, that I somehow knew, said, 'I love you too.'

"What gobbledygook are you speaking?"

"It's Romany, He understands it."

"Romany. That's gyppo talk."

"They are not gypsies!" She rounded on me. "They are Romany, gypsies are horrid people. But I am worried they know that I live here and will find us. I was frightened of this. That's why we left their camp that day as soon as I discovered one of the women there was my mum's sister. All gypsies are related you know. Come here," then we kissed for twenty minutes.

"I do love you, and things are happening at home. I have to go to Oxford with mum to see the university, meet the heads and find somewhere to stay. You must come and live up there, then we will always be together."

"I must see," I said. "It's not that easy to just go and live up there, but I will look into it."

She gave me a huge hug.

"Go on; look into it Ox, now." She whistled up Kicker and jumped up on his back forgetting her tummy pains and cantered off. I stood watching as she came to the corner to go down to the end of the orchard, but instead Kicker and her jumped the hedge in their stride and vanished.

I still blame myself for not telling Mandy the truth of the pony sooner, for on the following morning her father and brother were admitted to Ashford Hospital in a critical condition. Some visitors to the farm had beaten both of them senseless earlier in the day. Mandy's mum did not know whom they were, where they came from or recognised any of them. She could not even give a description of any of the six men, whether they were in suits or rags, she knew nothing. It was a funny do all round. Even the reason remained a mystery; why should anyone just turn up with bats of wood and try to kill them? The police wanted to know. I got this information on Thursday evening. It had happened while Mandy was at school on Wednesday and Sally had only heard today.

"How was Mandy?" I asked Sally, her safety first in my mind.

"Fine," she said, "seeming rather pleased as if it was what she wanted to happen to them." Sally thought it odd the way she seemed pleased but had no clue as to why. The thought crossed my mind that it may have something to do with all the beatings Mandy's parents had given her over the years. If the true father had turned up and spoken to Mandy's dad, and got the idea of how they treated her perhaps they had handed out their own kind of Gypsy punishment.

We said goodbye and I hung up wondering what was going on up at that house. I guessed it was the gypsies who had called and were they after the girl, Mandy? If so it was lucky she was at school I was scared for her safety. I had to find out; it could not wait. Father and brother in hospital, how could I see Mandy and warn her? There was only one way, the train trip from Ashford to her station of Appledore. So the next day at two pm, I took the train from Rye to Ashford, holding a return ticket to come back on the school train. A pair of old coaches and one engine in reverse, we called it the Doleham Flyer, still steam powered in these days. I was dressed in my best suit as a disguise in case I was spotted talking to Mandy as Alan's brother had been. From what my girl had said over the months I had known her, no love was lost with her father, and as Sally said on the phone, Mandy seemed pleased that her father was hospitalised. So I was confident that she would not go to the hospital to see him but catch this train. Sure enough there she was, her hair standing out amidst all the other school kids, aged from twelve to eighteen. Mandy's presence stated the fact that 'here I am!' She saw me from the other end of the platform, her dark eyes missing nothing. Holding her straw school hat on her head, she ran to me and put her arms around my neck.

"Darling! Fancy meeting you here! Come here," and we entered a coach at the engine end.

"Mandy. We must talk. How are you?"

"Fine," she said, and kissed me again.

"No stop that. Someone will see."

"I don't care. I am so happy! "

This was the jolly Mandy I knew, so different from the other day.

"How are your dad and brother? Sally phoned last night."

"Fine," she said, they will live. I wish I had been there when they gave him a hiding."

"Who?"

"I don't know," she said. In a tone of voice as if trying to hide her joy. Her relief of seeing me had meant her forgetting her home life for the moment. "I don't know anything," "The police haven't sent you have they?" I felt a shiver run all over my body.

"The police? Me? God no! Why? Do they know about us?"

"No, and they mustn't," she said. "You have never seen me, they are treating it as attempted murder, and mum is under suspicion. Can you meet me tonight, as they have mum in the station, at six at the usual place." The train gave a jolt and we were off. The other girls in our carriage were all agog and Mandy said "she had better introduce me to them. They all knew I was her boyfriend and could be trusted." I knew none of them and they all got off at Hamstreet, leaving Mandy and me on our own. Too soon Appledore came and I hid on the floor as Mandy alighted, saying, "See you at six, don't be late".

The train took an age to leave before I could get up and peer out of the window, but Mandy had vanished.

"Rye", the man on the platform announced, and I took my leave of British Rail and came home. Soon I was up on the farm standing under that old tree. The night was cold; a frost breathed on the plough and turned the turf white that stood out like icing sugar in the moonlight as the full moon of November tried to outshine the star studded sky. The mellow tone of the tune Mandy was singing came to me and I was able to pick out the pair's form from five hundred yards away as she strolled across the field to the jump into our cherry orchard. The night was cold and still; the breath came from the animal's nostrils in great clouds as he approached me. Mandy looked beautiful even under all the clothes she wore the old long overcoat fell from her shoulders to cover her legs and feet, her hair tied up in a large red scarf.

"You are early," she said as I greeted her.

"So are you!" she said. "Cold tonight."

"Yes," I said, "but how come you are out early tonight?"

"Mum said it would do me good after all that's gone on. The police let her home this morning on bail to look after my sister. She is one of their top suspects but they don't have enough to hold her on. It's cold. Can't we go to one of your sheds?"

"Ok," I said, "Come on. I'll beat you there. No-one will see us."

"I know," she said. "My big brother won't be around for a long time and mum has to look after the house with the kids. We're free!"

I started to run across the frost hard ground, through a gap in the hedge the other side of the large field to take a short cut up through the apple orchard, as Mandy set out to circumnavigate the field to reach the big apple orchard and sheds. I flung the doors open as the pair arrived, and Kicker clattered over the concrete floor, intent on getting his head into the sacks of corn that were standing in rows across the shed. Mandy reined him in and asked me to give her a hand getting off the saddle.

"What's the matter darling, you need a hand to get down?"

"It's my belly it really hurts, Kicker slipped just now and I slid forward in the saddle and hurt my self, but don't worry it is nothing."

I took her slim waist in my hands and lowered her to the floor she gave a gasp.

"What's the matter?" I said, as she straightened up.

"It is nothing just bellyache."

"No you don't!" she said, and led Kicker away from the corn, tying him up to a beam of wood. "If he got at that lot," she said, "he could kill himself."

In the dark interior of the shed over the other side, were a thousand new corn sacks that had been delivered to replace the ones the corn merchant had bought full from us. This was where we made for, hand in hand, and soon we were snugly covered over with Hessian sacks and Mandy's greatcoat, I enquired as to how her father was.

"His head is made of stone," she said. "He should be dead; they reckon he will make a full recovery, but my brother will never walk again without a limp. His poaching days are over they gave him a real pasting."

"Who?" I said.

"I don't know that!" she snapped back, "but I think mum does and so do the police, but she won't say. I don't know who they were and don't want to, but mum said they saw Kicker in the field, that's how they found us. Now don't worry; I am free for a while. Where are you taking me this week? I'm staying at Sally's. Mum said it was the best thing, to get away for a day or two. I shall go from school tomorrow and stay until mum says the coast is clear. She thinks they will be back. I'm cold, hug me." And after a few minutes she said,

"My belly is hurting; it's the cold please cuddle me and make the pain go away. We only lay beneath the pile for a few minuets before a grimace on her face told me all was not well with Mandy.

"Sorry darling, I will have to go home, but don't worry, we are free. I will see you tomorrow won't I, at Sally's? I will be there at four thirty. Come on, let's go." We surfaced and the frost hit us on the cheeks; our breath left our mouths in huge clouds. It was the worst frost of this winter. Mandy got up in the saddle with a leg up from me and leaned over to kiss me. I had to fight my way through the pile of hair as it cascaded over onto my head. She gave me a kiss, flung Kicker's head around and trotted out into the moonlight. I shut the doors and walked across the orchard to stand on the bank of the deep gill to watch her trot around the orchard and then walk up the headland of the now solid plough in the moonlight.

It was too frozen to trot; the pony had to feel its way. Her voice drifted across to me as she sang *'our love was on the wind. Now the wind has changed, winter is here, goodbye my love; the swallows have gone.'*

I stood and listened until she was out of sight and her voice was silent. The birds in the trees would now hear her as she walked Kicker alongside the wood and climbed the bank to her home. Tomorrow she was to be at Sally's. I was cold standing there so I jogged to the car and lit a fag, then turning the heater on full blast started to melt the frost from the windscreen, but had to give it a hand with a matchbox and scrape it off the outside. Mandy had asked me again for a hand to get off her mount, other times she had flung her body at me, some thing was amiss.

Tomorrow night could not come fast enough. It was early yet so I popped into the Bell Inn on my way home. Who should be there but Alan?

"John! You are still alive! How is Mandy? I heard the heavy boys turned up and killed her dad, mum and her brother. Everyone is on about it!"

"No Alan! Someone gave him and his son a good hiding, that's all. They are in hospital but will live. Wherever did you get that story from?"

"Dad," he said. "He was Mandy's way and the police stopped him and interrogated him in case he saw anyone; it had just happened." Alan went on and on. "Dad said it was none too soon, and mum told him to keep quiet, they know nothing, but I'm sure dad and mum know something. Its real cloak and dagger stuff, a big robbery or something; I bet it's stashed on the farm and the old man has done the dirty on the gang!"

"Oh do shut up Alan; you know nothing about it, and I warn you, you don't want to, so shut up!" It was my turn to tell him to warn him. He took the hint and never spoke of it again. That night I left the pub at ten thirty and went home.

CHAPTER TWELVE

Next day I was at Land Farm by five thirty, "just in time for tea," as Shirley put it. "Must have smelt the kettle boiling." I took a seat alongside Mandy; she was looking tired and was very quiet, not like the girl I was now in love with.

"Where are you going tonight?" Mrs. Wilton said, as we ate tea.

"We have been invited to a friend's at Hamstreet," said Mandy. "John met her on the train yesterday." Mrs Wilton showed no interest in my meeting she was now used to our surprise ways of communicating.

"Well, don't be late home will you and the straw barn is now full so be careful." I swallowed hard; she knew of the straw barn!

"It's very cold again tonight. Now John, don't let her get cold; she is looking rather peaky. I think she is catching a cold." Mrs. Wilton then went over, lifted one of Mandy's eyelids and looked into her eye. "You don't look well Mandy. Do you feel OK?" "Yes, fine."

"She had bellyache last night," I said. Then I realised what I had said. I was getting concerned now over Mandy's condition. Mrs Wilton did not know we had seen each other the previous night.

"That's it," Mrs. Wilton said. "Stood out in that cold, got you in the belly didn't it? You must be more careful John. Don't go getting her cold."

Mandy came down the stairs all dressed up in her pencil skirt and a pair of red four inch high heel shoes that she had bought in Ashford on her way home from school, with the money left over from the day she went shopping with Sally and Mary in Rye. I was so lucky to have a film star type of girlfriend.

"You approve?" she said to me, now looking me straight in the eyes and smiled as only Mandy could. Sally had cut her friend's fringe straight across the brow of Mandy's head. She looked like a Madonna with a mischievous smile that said, 'Come hither, let's love!' We followed Sally to the car as Mandy tottered to the door, gaining confidence with every step and once she had the balancing act over, was able to walk with ease. She sat in the car and swung her legs in. I shut the door and got behind the wheel.

"Where to?" I said, never thinking the story of a friend's house was true.

"Hamstreet, by the railway arch. Do you know it?"

"Yes," I said.

"It's the third house down," she said.

"So we are going to a friend's?" I said.

"Yes, I told you; she was on the train; don't you remember? She wears glasses with white rims, has dark hair in a perm."

"I'm sorry," I said. "There were so many pretty girls there."

"Cut the pretty out," she said. "You're mine! Now behave yourself! I expect there will be one or two of them there as Lizzy's mum and dad are away for the night." The road shone in the full moon, and the frost sparkled like minute mirrors. Soon we were at the house and Mandy sent me ahead to make sure it was the right one. Mandy elected to sit in the warm car with Sally while I went to knock on the door, it was answered by a girl with a perm in her brown hair and a pair of white wire rim glasses.

"Ox," she said. "How nice to see you again. Where's Mandy?"

"Where do you think?" said Mandy. "Left out in the bloody cold!" Mandy was trying to get to her feet on her stilettos and could swear if she wanted to! I ran to help her then we walked up the short path to the door, now framing three pretty faces.

"Look at Mandy!" one said, "What's she got around her neck?"

Her diamond and gold name glistened in the moonlight. "Goodness gracious! Where did you get all that from?"

The envy of the others soon disappeared when they remembered her home life that she had so often spoken of to them. After all they're teasing and gawping was over, we settled down to talk. A bottle of wine was opened and the four girls had a drink. I was bombarded with questions but the main topic was what were we going to do when Mandy went to university? I had already made up my mind on that score, and now seemed a good time to tell Mandy, the love of my life, I was going with her and hoped to wed the girl in future. Meanwhile I would support her in the custom to which she was becoming used to with me. Mandy, who had been quietly sitting with her arm around me, turned her face to look at me and burst into tears.

"You want to marry me?" and I dropped to one knee.

"Please Mandy; will you take me as your husband?" The tears now came bigger and faster.

"Darling, I love you. Yes, yes, yes!"

"OK, once will do. That's all that's needed!" said one of the open mouthed girls. "This calls for a drink. I'm sure daddy won't mind," and Lizzy got to her feet and fetched a bottle of cherry brandy from the side cupboard. Mandy hugged me; we then stood as they drank a toast to us both.

"I must ring and tell mum," said Sally. "She will be so thrilled. Only the other day she was saying the quicker Mandy gets out of her home, the better."

"A ring?" one of the girls said.

"Have you got a ring?"

"Of course not,' I said. "That comes next. Mandy must pick that," She looked at me through her water filled eyes.

"Darling you know nothing of me, I love you so much but I will be terrible to live with. Tomorrow," she said. "I can miss school for that. I'm only making up time for uni. I do not do anything new at school; I only go to get away from dad." One of the girls chipped in.

"You don't have to go to school at all now he's in hospital do you?"

"We will go to Maidstone where I got that," and pointed to her necklace and I got a bigger hug; I liked it. Mandy eighteen and me aged twenty. I was getting married and I wondered what mum and dad would say, to say nothing of the prophecy that old Charlie had made to dad, when I had asked for the day off work to take Mandy out. He had said, "Wedding bells next?" and given me that wink. Mandy dried her face and asked if I had a cigarette as her tummy was hurting and she wanted a smoke. One of the girls gave her one of theirs, and Mandy drew the first few puffs deep into her lungs, like the day she had that first smoke that I had given her, when we met under the old lime tree. Mandy made a face as if in pain and Lizzy looked at her.

"Why don't you go upstairs and have a lie down on my bed. You will feel much better in a while. It is the shock and why don't I go as well we were nearly married anyway."

So I took Mandy to our very first bed. The joy she showed as she lay down and relaxed, her red shoes abandoned on the floor.

"Put the light out and join me," said Mandy. So we lay on the bed together and cuddled and kissed. There we leant for the first time that the dress she was wearing was not the kind that lent itself to wooing.

"Wait a second, she said and slipped off the bed and removed her dress. I took my shirt and trousers off and layback alongside her, I started to touch her where she liked, her skin felt warm smooth and soft. My hand wandered and Mandy kissed me and relaxed, my embrace brought a gasp from her. I moved my hand and it felt wet and sticky.

"You're all wet and sticky Mandy?" I said, and got a nasty rebuke from her. She placed her hand down to mine, then pulled it back rapidly and put the bedside light on. The sight hit the two of us at the same time; all idea of making love for the first time vanished. There was blood everywhere. Mandy screamed I was out of the bed in record time. Where was it coming from? The convulsions from Mandy made me realise it was serious. I ran down the stairs two steps at a time to find the girls shouting, "Help! Mandy's bleeding bad!" Three girls took the stairs two steps at a time and that was going uphill! The sight of the blood on my leg and hand was the fuse for action. A girl passed me coming down for the phone as I was making my way back up to see what I could do and what was going on, only to be met by my trousers flying at me from one of the girls up above.

"Get them on now and get the ambulance quick!"

"My God, an ambulance! What was wrong? The girls would not let me in the room to see. I took myself out into the bitterly cold night air to wait for the bone wagon to arrive. It soon came with its light on top flashing and its bell ringing. The two attendants went into the house and I was told to wait in the sitting room. Soon the crying girls followed the ambulance men down the stairs with a stretcher on which lay my Mandy, only her head and necklace showing from the blanket as they took her out of the door. The moon shone on my girl and she smiled at me. "Kiss me darling; I'm sorry, so sorry it's not your fault."

The driver of the ambulance came round from the back after shutting the doors and looked at me.

"You should be ashamed of yourself how could you treat a girl like that, you are old enough to take more care." Alan's and the doctor's words came flooding back to me, 'Take care of Mandy.' What had I done? The girls were in tears. Sally came up to me and put her arm around me.

"Don't worry; she's in safe hands."

"What have I done?" I said.

"Nothing. It is a girl thing; don't worry. Now can you take me home please John, I must see mum; she will know what it is that's wrong with Mandy?" We said goodbye to the other three tearful girls and left. They were busy getting the bedclothes off the bed to wash. Mandy's shoes lay where she had slipped them from her feet and the pencil dress lay forlorn were she had let it drop. On getting into the car Sally placed her arm around my shoulder and we drove across the marsh to her house. All the way her arm was around my neck and she kept pressed her cheeks to mine but she would not tell me the reason for Mandy's pain or blood, it was 'a girl thing'. We arrived back at Land Farm and went in to see Shirley who was watching TV.

"You are home early. Where's Mandy?" Then Sally lost it. Her mother listened to it all and then Mr. Wilton, who had not spoken a word, looked at his wife.

"I told you so Shirley."

"Shut up. We are not talking to you; we don't know what is the matter. I am going to phone the hospital. Then we may know more." The hospital would tell Mrs. Wilton nothing and they said the girl did not want visitors, only her diary. Sally and Shirley were very upset so after a cup of tea, Sally got the locked diary that Mandy always updated when she came to stay. The diary lay on the table for Mrs. Wilton and Sally to deliver to the hospital the next day, as I left that night. They were sure Mandy would wish to see them, they would phone me tomorrow and perhaps if Mandy was still there, I could take Sally to see her

"Congratulations on getting engaged earlier." said Shirley and she gave me a hug as I left. They were both thrilled; 'we were a match made in heaven,' she said and 'don't worry Mandy would be fine'. They never got to see Mandy as at midnight the police came to their farm, demanded the locked diary and gave them a receipt for it. The secrets of the diary were for a long time never to be revealed to us and Mandy was isolated. What she suffered from was a mystery.

Mandy's parents' farm was sold and the family moved out within a week. No word came from Mandy but the hospital assured Mrs. Wilton that the girl had not died and was in fine health. Apart from that we knew nothing. I met the new owners of the farm but they knew nothing of the tenants before them. I never gave up hope that one day, my girl would somehow show herself to me beneath that old lime tree as I cultivated the fields.

I lost touch with Sally. We had nothing in common and she

had Martin. I saw her a few times at dances and we talked but she knew nothing, and Alan, the one who knew everything the day after Mandy and I had done it, he had no idea. Another robbery? Or maybe the police had found the stash from the last raid and they were all now rotting in jail. I was not to know that on that night, now so long ago, it would be the last time I ever saw My Mandy; it was as if she had never existed.

The years rolled by and every time I heard the song 'our love was on the wind, now the wind has changed', a tear formed in my eye. That was the last song I heard Mandy's wonderful voice sing that night of the full moon as she on her pony trod around that frozen plough and I wondered had the pony slipped and the saddle's pommel done her a terrible mischief? Then one Sunday morning came a phone call at nine am. Not the usual thing for a Sunday; must be trouble I thought as I picked the handset up.

"Hello. Can I speak to John Tiltman," the female voice on the other end said.

"Speaking," I said.

"John! It's Sally, how nice to hear you. It's been six and a half years. I did not know if you still lived there still. How are you?"

"Well," I said, "and you?"

"Very well," she said, "Have you seen the News of the World this morning?"

"No," I replied.

"Well you must she said. It's Mandy! You do remember Mandy and the pony?"

"Remember!" I said. "Of course, I loved her, I still do and dream of her? What's she in the paper for? She is all right isn't she?"

"Yes. Get the paper," and "We must see each other tonight. What are you doing tonight?"

"Tonight?"

"Yes, tonight! We must meet. I only live in Ashford. You know the Woolpack on the Marsh at Brookland? Meet you there at seven thirty. Now read the paper and don't be late," and she put the phone down. Mandy in the News of the World I thought, 'a paper of slush and vulgarity,' my mother always called it. Whatever was it? I needed a copy and now, so I hurried to the car and shot off down to the local paper shop in the village. A local girl in that paper would surely cause a stir and a queue. I was surprised to find the shop empty and Mr. Burt behind the counter reading the football results."

"Hello John. Don't usually see you in here on a Sunday. What can I get you?"

"Have you got a copy of the News of the World?"

"Of course, did you know the girl?" he said in a matter of fact sort of way. He had obviously read it. I knew nothing, especially as I knew nothing of the news.

"There we are," he said, "Front and centre pages." The headlines stood out. **FIFTEEN YEARS FOR FATHER, EIGHT YEARS FOR MOTHER. BROTHER RELEASED FOR LACK OF EVIDENCE.** There were photos of Mandy's mum and dad. God! I ordered and paid for two papers then hurriedly left the shop to sit in the car and read the paper. Alan was right I thought they have been caught, I sat in the car and looked at the text, a shudder ran through me and I went cold. It was nothing of the sort. I started to read on but the tears in my eyes made me stop, and I could not carry on reading. Surely there was some kind of mistake.

That week history was made when the first case of the victim took her parents and brother to the Old Bailey. The mother was jailed for aiding and abetting. It had been going on since the girl had been six years of age now the girl had graduated into one of the only women barristers to take silk and prosecute her own family. The court had stood up and applauded on hearing the verdict and the paper went on and on with all the sordid details. I could not read any more; they were talking of my love, all those times she had said.

"Go on have me. I know how to please you." It had been brainwashed into her by her father, and mother.

I sat in the car and cried. My Mandy! They were talking about my little Kentish maid, the loving girl who rode that pony. The girl I called my Moon Girl. All that time and she never told me. It all now made some sort of sense. I dried my eyes and thought of tonight. I had a few questions for Sally at the Woolpack. I arrived early and entered to order a coffee, and found a table to place the paper on. Sally was not far behind me.

"John!" she said, on seeing me, and put her arms around me, giving me a big hug.

"Your Mandy! What a girl. This is my husband. You remember Martin?" And he shook my hand.

"A nasty business this," he said, pointing to the paper on the table, folded to hide the headlines from the other customers.

"Take a seat Sally. How are your mum and dad?" I said.

"They will be here in a moment," she said. "They must see you."

"What?"

"I'll let them explain," she said.

"Sally. Did you know? I must know; did you know? Did you have any suspicions at all?

"No, honestly John; do you think I would have let it go on if I had known? Poor Mandy." Then Mrs. and Mr. Wilton walked in; Shirley nearly threw herself at me.

"My dear boy!" she said. "I never knew, I really never knew it was as bad as that," she started to cry, which moistened my eyes as well.

"Why did she not say?" I said,

"It seems that girls seldom do," she said. "I have been speaking to a nurse, a friend of mine, she says it is always the step father. Have you not read the paper"?

"No, I couldn't," I said.

"You must," she said. "It throws so much light on the whole rotten sordid family. Sit down," and she sat by my side and cuddled me to her as her husband talked at the bar to his daughter and son in law. "You have not read it? You can read can't you?"

- 132 -

"Of course," I replied. Only it's my Mandy, and I burst into tears. Shirley took me in her arms and cuddled me. "I know it is terrible but it is all over now. Put the paper away read it later when the shock wears off," pushing the paper on the table towards me. "I will tell you what it says, Mandy was not the child of the dad she knew, but sometime after her big brother was born, her dad and mother had an argument. Mandy's mum had gone back to the gypsy camp and got herself pregnant. She had then gone back home to her husband and the child was born, Mandy, his step child?"

"Yes." I said, "I knew he was not her real dad."

"Well later he started to interfere with Mandy. You know what I mean don't you?"

"Yes. He's the one who hurt her?"

"Yes, but in more ways than you could see. It upsets a girl of that age and they are terrified to say anything. Then when Mandy told her mum, she told Mandy to shut up. It was their custom of men to use women when they wanted. Mandy was brainwashed until you came along," and she gave me another of her big hugs.

"Mandy stated in so many words in her report to the court that it was an eighteen year old boy called Ox who showed her true love and refused to violate her young body." She gave me another hug,

"That was you. She called you Ox didn't she? I'm blaming myself; my husband said there was something amiss and I would not let him speak because if he was wrong, it is a terrible thing to be blamed for, and poor Mandy; that is why she studied law, so she could blow the lid off the whole sordid thing and protect her young sister from suffering the same fate.

It was when you turned up that Mandy started to realise the wrong he was up to."

"But why did she not tell me?" She hugged me, "You must not blame yourself," she said. "We are all guilty, even Alan's parents."

"Alan's mum and dad? Did they know, what did they say?"

I haven't seen them lately," she said.

"Only Alan always said his mum and dad had arguments over Mandy's family, his mum told him to keep his mouth shut. It seems a lot of people had their suspicions. Sally is really hurt. She says you should have known." I interrupted her,

"I had so many people telling me to be careful, even a doctor once."

"A doctor?" Shirley blurted out

"Yes. When we went that time to a barbecue, Mandy got stung."

"Yes I remember."

"Well a doctor in the pub looked at her and later came up to me, telling me to be more careful and not hurt her. He saw the bruises. I never did because we always met at night in the moonlight. Mandy tried to tell me herself in the straw shed down your farm but never could admit something so horrible, even to herself. Now the way she spoke and acted makes sense." Mrs. Wilton hugged me close to her, "You poor lad".

"You must not blame yourself. You saved the girl. Be thankful for that," and "Mandy will never have to look for work again. They will be knocking her door down to get her to work for them. She will go far. Who else could you wish for to represent you than a girl like her? She's been there and won. Her diary you know had all the dates and times he raped her. That was why she kept them locked up at our house. If only I had known."

All five of us sat talking until we were asked to leave. I drove home that night with tears in my eyes, and slept in spells, not being able to put my 'Moon Girl' out of my head. If only I had known more about the opposite sex, then maybe I would have seen that the way she acted was out of character for girls. But darling Mandy had been my first love. The next day I made a point of going to the shallow depression at the edge of the field that the sheep's grave had left by the wire fence and cried.

The following week another paper carried the story and a picture of the woman who was now famous, she looked out at me from the paper, her jet-black hair much shorter, but her dark eyes the same, 'all seeing and knowing' and around her neck was her name in gold and diamonds. '**MANDY**.'

THE END

Printed in the United Kingdom
by Lightning Source UK Ltd.
102971UKS00001B/244-354